9/20

TUNE It OUT

Jamie Sumner

Atheneum Books for Young Readers
New York London Toronto Sydney New Delhi

ATHENEUM BOOKS FOR YOUNG READERS

An imprint of Simon & Schuster Children's Publishing Division

1230 Avenue of the Americas, New York, New York 10020

ATHENEUM BOOKS FOR YOUNG READERS is a registered trademark of Simon & Schuster, Inc. Atheneum logo is a trademark of Simon & Schuster, Inc.

For information about special discounts for bulk purchases, please contact Simon & Schuster Special Sales at 1-866-506-1949 or business@simonandschuster.com.

The Simon & Schuster Speakers Bureau can bring authors to your live event. For more information or to book an event, contact the Simon & Schuster Speakers Bureau at 1-866-248-3049 or visit our website at www.simonspeakers.com.

Book design by Karyn Lee

The text for this book was set in Adobe Garamond Pro.

Manufactured in the United States of America

0720 FFG

First Edition

2 4 6 8 10 9 7 5 3 1

Library of Congress Cataloging-in-Publication Data

Names: Sumner, Jamie, author.

Title: Tune it out / Jamie Sumner.

Description: First edition. | New York : Atheneum Books for Young Readers, 2020. | Audience: Ages 10 Up. | Audience: Grades 4–6. | Summary: Twelve-year-old Lou Montgomery's life has been centered on her mother's terrifying plan to make her a singing star, but a crisis reveals Lou's sensory processing disorder and people determined to help her address it.

Identifiers: LCCN 2019044635 | ISBN 9781534457003 (hardcover) | ISBN 9781534457027 (eBook)

Subjects: CYAC: Singers—Fiction. | Sensory disorders—Fiction. | Mothers and daughters—Fiction. | Custody of children—Fiction. | Theater—Fiction.

Classification: LCC PZ7.1.S8545 Tun 2020 | DDC [Fic]—dc23

LC record available at https://lccn.loc.gov/2019044635

For Paula Flautt,
the best theater teacher a girl could ask for

1
Bagels and Joe

Bagels and Joe can't be more than the size of your average motel room, but it is wall-to-wall jars of roasted coffee beans. It smells nutty and warm on this cold September morning. No one looks for a truant in a place like this. Ordinarily I love it here, curled up with a book and headphones in a corner where I can be any age at all in the low light. But today I can't hide. Because today I am the entertainment.

It's been a month since our last show and my most recent episode. I can still feel the terrible panic, hear the confused voices of the crowd, and see Mom trying to gather our money and run. I suppose I should be grateful for the four-week break with no shows along the lake. She has a job now too, at the diner down the road, so we've usually got enough leftover hash browns and day-old donuts to keep us fed. But that doesn't mean she still hasn't been trying, like always, to land me the "next big gig." And today we've got a show.

I can't tell if the time off has made the fear better or worse. Do I want to throw up more or less than I normally do before a performance? It's too close to call.

It doesn't help that Bagels and Joe is also "the place" to come in Lake Tahoe to find undiscovered talent. I can't believe Mom finally talked Joe, the owner, into it. Maybe he heard about what had happened in front of the restaurant. Everybody always feels sorry for me after they see me melt down.

That can't happen today. Mom's already given me the "stand tall, be brave, keep it together" speech. She also tacked on the "you have a gift to share with the world" speech for good measure. But there are *so many people* clinking cups and scraping forks on plates. They've crammed themselves around wobbly tables that Joe himself moved out through the open doors and onto the deck. I am standing with my back to it all, tuning Mom's guitar and swallowing buckets of air. No matter how many breaths I take, it's not enough. I feel light-headed and fluttery, like a paper caught on a fence.

The tuning is good. It gives my hands something to do. I won't be playing the guitar, though. That's Mom's job. Whenever it comes time to sing in front of people, I can't do anything but squeeze my hands tight behind my back. I used to close my eyes, too, but once I turned eleven, Mom said I had to keep them open or I'd creep out the customers. Good. Let them be as creeped out by me as I am by them. It's like the moment right before you're supposed to blow out the candles on your birthday cake, when all the pressure's on you. Except none of them can step in and help if I can't do it.

I look out over the railing. The lake and the sky are the same blue—so light they're almost white, and it makes me think of heaven. And rest and quiet. I tug at Mom's sleeve so she'll pull back from the audience she's currently "meeting and greeting."

"I want to start with the Patty Griffin song," I whisper. She nods without looking away from the couple in spandex active wear at the front table.

She jerks a glittery pink thumbnail toward them so only I can see. "Ray Bans and Rolexes," she says. "Today's the day, baby. I can feel it. Somebody in this pack is a scout from LA."

She stares at the couple, lazily stirring their coffees with tanned hands, like she's hungry for something that has nothing to do with food. My insides turn to soup, and I feel sloshy and heavy all at once. My suede jacket feels too tight. Like saran wrap that's shrinking. Joe gives me a thumbs-up over by the open doors. He's been nice, nice enough to let me sing on his property and to allow Mom in all her glory to put up flyers everywhere and basically boss his servers around all morning long. There's always some promising musician up here trying to get a Saturday spot on the deck. He must do pretty well. I bet he doesn't have to sleep in a truck like Mom and me. I shoot him a tiny smile.

Maybe this time will be different. At least out here on the deck, the customers are a good four feet away. No unexpected touches. I take a breath like I'm about to dive underwater as Mom starts to speak in the voice she saves especially for shows. She sounds like the ringmaster in a circus. Or a car salesman.

"Now this show is about to get under way, and we so appreciate your attendance. If you would, please hold your applause until the end. And *boy* will you want to applaud." She pauses and chuckles like she always does. "And now, the lovely Louise Montgomery!"

My insides have liquefied. But I hand Mom the guitar and watch her count off: "A one, a two, a one two three four—" and then I find it. One red spot on a pine branch five feet away, just above the heads of the spandex couple. It's a cardinal. And today he's going to be who I sing to so I don't have to look at the crowd. I fix my eyes on him, and as I do, he turns his tufted head toward me and our eyes meet and it is luck and it is just enough to get me going.

I let the beat of Mom's guitar strum through me

and start low, lower than a twelve-year-old girl should be able to go, or so Mom says. I sing of heaven and clouds and troubles blowing away in the wind.

I go high on the "trouble," and my cardinal friend cocks his head, like he knows I'm lying, because nothing chases away trouble. Except maybe the sound of my own voice in my head.

I close my eyes and let the music take me. I sing of sorrow and time I can't borrow, and too soon I feel a tightening in my gut over what I have to do when the song's over. I never want it to end. If I could sing forever, I would. Then I'd never have to speak to a living soul other than my mom.

I go so low on the last line that it feels like a secret to myself. I say it over and over. Finally, my voice quivers to a stop like a penny settling on a counter. When the applause hits, it's loud and sharp and knocks me back like a crack of thunder. The cardinal springs from his tree, and I drop to my knees. I *will not* rock back and forth. I *will not* whimper and whine. We can't have a repeat of what happened at Christy's. We can't. I bite my tongue until I taste blood.

I feel Mom come up behind me. She shoves the guitar at me and mutters, "Pretend like you're tuning." She's covering. Like she always does. She tosses her dyed blond hair over her shoulder and begins a speech mostly knit together with thank-yous. She takes her time asking for requests from the group, beaming most of her megawatt smile at the couple at the front table. I get myself under control.

By the time we begin the rest of our set, I am back to normal enough to finish three more songs. When the applause comes again, I stick my fingers in my ears while pretending to hold my hair back for a curtsy. I'm so relieved it's over I feel woozy.

Joe approaches with a cup of coffee. I take it and breathe it in. The foam and sugary sweetness hit me like smelling salts and bring me back to myself. I study Joe over my cup while he keeps an eye on the crowd. He's a muscly guy with tan lines from his sunglasses that make him look like a very nice raccoon. Right now, his arms are crossed like he's my own personal bodyguard. People give us space.

"Not bad, Louise. Not bad at all," he says once the

crowd begins to move back inside. "Your mom was right when she said you had the pipes."

I smile into my cup.

"Don't tell her I caffeinated a minor, okay?"

We both look over to where she's standing, her hands on the hips of her tightest black jeans, talking to the Ray Ban guy.

"I don't think she'd care."

"No?" Joe gives me a look like he wants to ask more. I've already said too much, gotten too comfortable. He's easy to talk to, and that's a problem. What happens between me and Mom stays between me and Mom.

I begin packing up the guitar and tasseled rug we unroll for performances.

"Thanks for the joe, Joe," I say.

"Was that a joke?" He makes a shocked "oh" face, and I laugh, because the caffeine has kicked in and I'm happy my job is done for the day. "I didn't think you had it in you. Stay cool, Louise," he says, and walks back into the café, throwing a dish towel over his shoulder.

Oh no. Mom is leading the fancy spandex couple over, and I immediately tense up. I guess I'm not quite done for the day after all.

Mom starts the introductions.

"Louise, I'd like you to meet Howard Maze."

"Howie. Please." Howie sticks out a big hand with stubby fingers. I can't do it. A shake is too much. I give a little wave instead. He doesn't seem to mind.

"This is my wife, Margaret. Maggie."

Howie and Maggie. Same height, same glasses, same dark hair. They could have been cartoon super-villains.

"We're a husband-and-wife talent team—the Maze Agency. We're a family business, and we're in the business of making families' dreams come true," Howie says like he's in a commercial. "And we love your sound."

"You've really got something, honey," Maggie chimes in, lifting her glasses and eyeing me up and down. "Kind of raspy, like a modern Stevie Nicks."

"A tiny dynamo, like Amy Winehouse," Howie adds.

"But fragile-looking," counters Maggie, "like early

Taylor Swift." This is too weird. I feel my jacket getting tight again. Mom nods. She's been following the two of them as they size me up like it's a tennis match. But I'm white-knuckling the coffee cup for all I'm worth. I can do this. I can be calm. Please, *please* don't let the Mazes try to touch me.

Just as Howie's reaching toward me like he wants to try that handshake again, Mom bumps Howie's shoulder with hers like they're old friends and says, "I told you you were in for a treat." He drops his hand as she keeps talking. "And this is just a taste. Wait until you hear her miked and in studio."

What is Mom doing? I study my toes while the three of them look at me. I have never set foot in a studio in my life. She's making promises I can't keep.

"Yeah, I believe it. I like her sound already. And the acoustics out here are zilch. I'm thinking commercial jingles at first. Then we'll talk singles. She's young yet. Does she act? Could she do Disney?"

The idea of television makes me want to puke. I consider puking right here to prove my point, but he keeps talking, more to himself than to us.

"Never mind, never mind," he says. "This is vacation, not business, and believe it or not, we like to keep the two separate."

It's the first thing he says that makes me think I might like Howie Maze. Maybe he really is a family guy, and it's not just a line? Disney's a joke. Commercials of any kind are a joke. There's no way a camera pointed at me would turn out well. But could I handle being alone in a studio? I picture it. A black box with nothing inside it but me and the music. It sounds soothing, like a sleeping bag zipped all the way up. But he ruins the dream with what he says next.

"We can't tell anything until we get her into our offices back in LA. We've got a studio there, and we'll see how she reads and looks on camera. Do you have a headshot?"

For just one second Mom looks as panicked as I feel. But then it's gone. "Ah no. Sorry, Howie. Left those on the plane, I'm afraid. It was a rough transfer from Chicago to Reno."

We have never been on a plane in our lives.

Maggie taps my shoulder, and I flinch. "Here, honey,

you take this." She hands me an ivory card with THE MAZE AGENCY printed on it in big blue letters. "Call us at the office, and we'll set something up when we get back." She turns to her husband, who is snapping to-go lids on both their lattes. "What do you think, Howie, end of next week?"

"Next week. Yeah, that should work. Vacation first, then work."

"Excellent. We'll check our schedule and get back to you," Mom says like we're on tour. But the Mazes are already making their way through the doors and back out into the Tahoe morning.

I swallow the last of my coffee and stare into the bottom of my cup. This was supposed to be free coffee and enough of a gig to keep Mom happy for another few weeks. Despite all her pep talks over the years, I never thought I'd actually have someone think I was good enough to sign. I love to sing because the sound of my own voice in my ears steadies me. It makes me feel stronger than I am. I try to imagine doing that in front of cameras and crowds and high fives and handshakes and applause. An acidy burp escapes my throat and burns. As soon as the Mazes disappear, I grab Mom's hand.

"Mom, we can't go to LA next week."

"Why not?" She's smiling and clicking her fingers together like there's a song playing I can't hear.

"Because . . . you have a job here. . . ." *Because I like the mountains and the quietness of this place,* I think. *Because if someone tries to fit me for a Disney costume, I will implode.*

"A job?" She stops and points to a stool so I'll sit. "You mean the minimum-wage, no-insurance, *waitress* job? Yeah, tough decision there."

I shake my head. I hate it when she gets sarcastic with me. The deck is almost empty now that the free entertainment's over. I move to set my cup on the stool next to me, and it wobbles because my hands are shaking again. She sees it and leans her shoulder, as carefully as always, into mine. I sigh with relief at the weight of it. If either of us were to pull away, we'd both topple over.

"It's about a seven-hour drive down to LA," she says in a low, calm voice. "How about this—we go next week, see what happens?" The way it comes out, she sounds like she couldn't care less if I get it or not. But I know better. "And then, hey, if they love you as much as I think they will, we'll sign a big contract, make this our home base, and fly back and forth like fancy jet-setters?"

There it is. Her not-so-secret Hollywood dream life. But I can't pretend I don't like the idea of making Lake Tahoe permanent.

"Like with a real house here, maybe?" I ask, against my better judgment. "One of those cabins by the water near Commons Beach?"

Mom smiles. "Why not, baby girl? You're a fighter, and you've fought your way almost to the tippity top. With your abilities, we could buy a McMansion in Beverly Hills."

I smile too, because if I ignore the whole performing-in-public part, I can kind of see it. Not the McMansion. I see the rich people who fly into Tahoe for the weekend, with their shiny SUVs and ten-dollar lattes. They've never clipped a coupon or wondered where they'd sleep at night. But they don't look any happier. I just want a little cabin with my own bedroom where I can pin pictures to the walls and pick out a quilt for the bed. We would have a kitchen—a real one, not a camp stove—and a refrigerator that would always be full. There'd be a path to the water, too. A place of my own.

"Hey, you two, lunch on the house?"

Joe comes out and hands me a bag with two bagel sandwiches and chips inside. I can smell the smoked salmon, and my stomach growls, yells really. It'll be the first thing I've eaten today. There were no freebies from Mom's late shift last night.

"Thanks, hon." Mom slides off the stool. "And thanks for letting my baby girl take the stage this morning."

"Sure. It was an honor. Louise, you've got a great voice. Keep at it."

Mom bobs her head in agreement like he's just stated the obvious—the sky is blue; the world is round; Lou's voice is great.

"Listen," Joe adds. "I know school's back in session, but I hope you find the time for your music. I really do."

Quick as I can, I drop my head and let the curtain of my hair fall forward. Mom made me memorize the name of the middle school in town, but I can't remember it. Why can't I remember it? Thank goodness for Mom. "Oh, she's a good manager of her time, Joe. A real responsible kid. Homework first, that's what I say, and singing second. And she sticks to it. Straight As all the way."

I sigh inside. She's gone too far. It's still too early in the year for grades, even *I* know that, but Joe either doesn't pick up on it or doesn't care, because he smiles when I squeak out a "Thank you for the lunch," and Mom pulls us away, through the café and back out onto the sidewalk. The sun isn't as warm as it was just a few weeks ago. October is almost here. How am I going to hide the fact that I'm not in school once the weather turns too cold to be outside? Not that I'm complaining. I love the mountain quiet where I can be alone without bells ringing and bus brakes screeching and kids bumping into me. I miss the homework, though. There's only so much you can learn from the donations in the Little Free Library. While we walk back down the hill to the campsite, Mom hums. School's the last thing on her mind.

I flip down the tailgate, and we sit in the bed of the

truck with our feet up and tucked into each other. The Chevy used to be white. It's more a dirty beige now with cracks of rust running through it. But it's home. I unwrap both our sandwiches, and we eat slowly, savoring something that's not fried or out of a can. I lick the cream cheese off my fingers and then tip the paper wrapping up to catch the last of the crumbs. Right now, this is just about perfect. It's cozy in the truck, and there's a couple trying to teach their little kid to fish. He keeps throwing his Elmo pole into the water when he casts his line. It's hilarious.

Mom reaches over and tucks a piece of hair behind my ear. I smell her, the warm tanned scent of her underneath the cigarette smoke. She moves to grab a Camel from her stash, but I catch her hand and hold it. She shakes her head but laughs.

"Maybe now's the time to quit. A fresh start for me and you. Yeah?" she says.

I nod into her shoulder, and we both shiver when a gust of wind blows in off the lake.

"It's colder now than it was this morning." She sighs. "It's probably eighty degrees in LA. What do you bet?"

I don't answer. Instead, I scooch down so my head is on her lap. She moves her fingers through my hair slowly, and it doesn't make me want to twitch. She's the only one who can touch me like this without making me jump or cringe. There's no startle reflex when it comes to her. I close my eyes and remember when I was littler and she used to do it all the time. . . .

It was the year I turned ten, and we lived down in Biloxi. We were hitting the casino circuit then. Mom had a job at a souvenir shop selling maps and T-shirts and gator-teeth necklaces. The tourist season was steady enough, even after the Katrina rebuild, that we could afford to stay at the Starlight, a pay-by-the-week motel just off the highway on a little strip of beach. I went to real school there too, all of fourth grade. Mom got me a Dora the Explorer backpack on discount from her work, and I ate a hot breakfast and lunch every day because the county paid. Biscuits and eggs and spaghetti and pizza and big, warm chocolate chip cookies. It was the longest I remember not being hungry.

It was also when I realized something was wrong

with me. "On the spectrum," I heard my teacher, Mrs. Guidry, whisper to another teacher at recess when I freaked out when a kid tried to push me on the swings. I didn't know what it meant. But when I asked Mom later, she got mad and didn't answer. Then I handed her a note from Mrs. Guidry and the school counselor. They wanted me to be tested. But Mom barely looked at it before tearing it into teeny-tiny pieces. She yelled that she was going to go down to the school to give them a piece of her mind. But she never did. We hit the road the next day. That was the end of Biloxi.

It was only later, after we'd moved, that I realized they'd meant autism. I've never been tested for it. Mom refused when they brought it up at school conferences. But I guess it didn't matter. My teachers had already decided. They treated me different, and so I felt more different than ever. They were the grown-ups, so they must be right.

Mom lived for the weekends in Biloxi, when we'd hit up the "karaoke for kids" nights at the Beau Rivage and Hard Rock and Treasure Bay—all the big casinos. I can still remember the air when you first walked in. It was blasting cold, like stepping into a giant refrigerator. I kept a fuzzy old sweatshirt in my backpack that Mom made me take off before I performed. She said it was cold because they pumped in extra oxygen so the gamblers would stay awake and keep spending money. I believe it.

The karaoke nights, though, those were bad. The strobe lights were so bright they left lightning streaks on the back of my eyelids when I blinked. And the kids were mostly older than me, already eleven or twelve, and they danced and sang, and it was all hip-hop or rap. I actually like rap, the kind that sounds like poetry and doesn't need instruments in the background to make you feel it in your bones. But Mom would pick Dolly Parton or a show tune from Grease, and I'd just stand there with my eyes closed and pull at the skin on my elbows while I sang. The only good thing about it was that no one really paid attention to what was happening onstage. Mom thought those karaoke nights would be our big break. She thought there'd be talent scouts. It took a whole year before she realized no one was looking for "the next big thing" in a karaoke club in Mississippi.

But after every show, when we were back in our room at the Starlight, I would take a bath and curl up in my towel on the bed. Mom would comb my hair out with her fingers just like she's doing now, and we'd watch something goofy on the television . . . old episodes of *Andy Griffith* or *Charlie's Angels.*

"Did you know I'm named after a Charlie's Angel, baby girl?" she said one night.

I sat up and twisted around in my towel so I could tell if she was joking or not, but she was looking at the screen.

"That one." She pointed to a woman with big blond hair and bell-bottom jeans. "Farrah Fawcett."

"Your name's Jill."

"Jill's her name on the show." Mom stopped playing with my hair and curled her skinny arms around her knees.

"Your grandma wanted a beauty queen for a daughter."

Mom could have been a beauty queen if she'd wanted. She's the most beautiful person I've ever seen—even more than the casino girls in their feathers and sequins. But she never talked about my grand-parents. All I knew was they'd kicked her out when she got pregnant with me at seventeen. "Hard to kick someone out of a double-wide I never wanted to be in in the first place," she'd say any time I brought them up. I learned not to ask. But I still tried to picture them, Ronald and Leslie Montgomery of middle-of-nowhere Arkansas. They're just blurred faces, though, all dis-torted like in a funhouse mirror. I guess that's pretty much what Mom sees too.

I feel Mom's hand still on my head and I sit up. I miss Biloxi. Not the casinos with their jangling noises and bright lights and carpet that smelled like beer and ciga-rette ash, but I miss the school with its steady meals and the Starlight with a clean bed and a bath.

Maybe Mom's right. Maybe this *will* be different. Maybe I won't freak out like I did in front of Christy's restaurant when the crowd got too close, pushing me in on all sides. I can still feel the way the gravel dug into my knees after I screamed and dropped to the ground. I can still hear their voices:

"Is she okay?"

"What happened?"

"I just touched her. That's it. And she . . . screamed."

"Drugs, you think?"

"Too young."

"No such thing as too young."

"That's a little cynical."

"Well, whatever it is, someone needs to do something about that mother."

And above it all, Mom yelling, "Get your hands off my daughter!"

I shake my head. Maybe Howie and Maggie will like me so much they'll offer me a job, and I can sit in a dark, quiet studio and make some music *and* some money, and it'll be better for both of us. I'll turn into the star, and the fighter, Mom thinks I already am.

2

I'm On My Way

We're meeting with the Mazes on Friday. It's Wednesday afternoon. That's about a million too many minutes to kill. There's not much to pack up when you live in a truck, and we're leaving first thing in the morning after Mom gets off late at the diner. She's been pulling double shifts for the last week. We'll need every cent for gas money and a place to stay. I don't think there are many campsites in the woods in LA.

As I'm walking up the hill, I wish I had more than this sweatshirt on. It's cold today. The clouds are lumps of heavy ash waiting to drop. I can smell the coffee and something cinnamony up at Joe's, though, so I keep going. I want to say good-bye to him, but it's against the rules. Mom said we can't let anyone know we're leaving town, so we don't get too many questions about how we can just pick up and leave so fast. But that doesn't mean I can't *see* him. I'm saying hello, not good-bye.

When I walk in, Joe leans on the counter with a dish towel over his shoulder like a bartender. "No school today?"

Oh. I'd been so focused on not breaking the "good-bye rule" that I forgot I'm technically supposed to be in school. But after Mrs. Guidry in Biloxi, Mom decided I'd never go back. She said, "Life's too short to get hung up on your weak spots, baby. Let's focus on your talents." And that was that.

"No, uh, out sick. Nothing contagious, just, uh, the throat, you know?" I manage a tiny cough.

"Well, we've got to protect that voice. How about some tea?"

I nod and sit at a stool at the far end of the counter

where no one can bump against me. I just really don't like being touched. Sometimes not even by Mom. I never have. Loud noises, too—those are bad, maybe worse. I've never seen a fireworks show in my life. Well, that's not entirely true. When I was four, I saw about thirty seconds of one from a rooftop of a crummy apartment building in Conway, Arkansas, but that's all it took. Cue the screams, the hair pulling, the biting. Yeah, I used to bite—myself, not other people, although I'm not sure that's better.

Luckily, I've outgrown a few of my worst "quirks," as Mom likes to call them. Which means today, when Joe passes me the tea, I do not flinch when our fingers accidentally touch (even though I want to). Instead, I stick my face over the steam and let it thaw. My nose is beginning to run by the time he gets back with a honeypot so small it looks like it came from a toy tea set. *I'm going to miss that honeypot,* I think, and my throat closes up. If Joe catches me crying, he's going to think I'm a nutcase.

"Here, you." He passes me a napkin to wipe my nose, which is embarrassing, but I do it anyway. I sip

my tea and watch Joe hand a lady her change at the register. He has kind eyes. But Howie has kind eyes too. Maybe it will be okay. And if Mom keeps her promise, LA isn't forever. We'll be back.

"Everything all right, Lou?"

"Yeah, just, you know, under the weather." I pull the cuffs of my sweatshirt down around my hands and stare into my cup. There was a woman in Biloxi, Miss Margie, who used to read tea leaves. She'd dump them out and stir them around with her finger and then tell you whether you'd meet the love of your life, or if a big change was coming, or if you should buy that alligator purse on sale. I wonder what she'd say if I passed her this cup right now?

Joe starts wiping the counter right in front of me. It's perfectly clean. He wants to talk. That can't happen. I take one last swig of tea and hop down from my stool.

"Well, you take care of yourself, okay?" he says. "And tell your mom to stop by and we'll get you booked for another show. The winter tourist season will be picking up soon."

"Okay." I dig a bunch of change from my pocket and hold it up. "Here." I hope it's enough.

"Uh-uh." He waves it off. "On the house. Now get on home before it gets any later. Weather Four said there's some snow blowing in."

"Thanks. I will." I walk to the door. I keep my promise to Mom. I don't say good-bye. But I let myself look around for a second to memorize this place and Joe, just in case.

By the time I get back to the truck, I'm freezing again, and there are little flecks in the air, not really snow, just tiny whispers of it, like dust the wind kicks up. I climb into the back and turn on the portable heater before crawling into my sleeping bag fully clothed. I eat a package of Cheetos and drink some water. But the wind is blowing so hard off the lake, it's making the truck canopy creak and grind, and I can't settle. I try reading my old dog-eared copy of *The Hunger Games*, but it's getting dark, and I don't want to turn on a light in case it draws attention. Finally, I zip my sleeping bag all the way up and bury my head and try to sleep.

I'm dreaming of a farm, one we visited once in Kentucky. I'm little, four or five maybe, and wading through a sea of strawberries. The ground is soft, like sand. When it collapses under my sandals, I drop my bucket. The berries go rolling. I cry. Mom swoops in to hand me one. It's perfect, red all the way around and warm from the sun. The juice runs down my chin and onto my T-shirt, and we laugh, sitting in the dirt in the middle of the Kentucky heat.

The buzzing sneaks up on me until it's so loud, I jerk upright. It's the alarm. 11:48 p.m. I'm late.

Mom's about to get off her shift. The heater's gone off, and I'm freezing in the pitch black. I can see my breath in the air, like I'm a ghost. I throw the suede jacket over my sweatshirt and pop the tailgate. The world is white. The storm came while I was sleeping.

I hop down, careful not to slip, and my feet crunch in the snow. In this light, it sparkles. I shiver and wipe my nose and let the glow of the moonlight on the water and the snow light my way to the truck's cab. I climb in the driver's-side door, grab the keys, and start the engine. I find an old towel on the floorboard and use it to wipe the snow from the windshield as best I can. I'm due to pick Mom up in fifteen minutes.

We talked it all out ahead of time. With the double shifts and no bus service, I have to be the one to pick her up. It's no big deal, only a few miles down the road. I've been driving since I was ten. I just have to be careful not to get spotted. Though I've never driven in snow. My insides curl up like dead leaves on a tree, but we leave for LA in six hours. Mom's counting on me.

Once the windshield's mostly clear, I get back in, adjust the seat, and check my mirrors, just like Mom taught me. It's a pretty straightforward drive to the diner. Just head out of the campsite and make a right on Grove Street and follow it all the way there. But the snow's so new and it's so late that when I pull out onto the road, I can't even see the double yellow lines.

My hands are shaking. I'm going *maybe* ten miles an hour. I'm afraid to go faster. I turn on the radio to help me concentrate. It's an Ed Sheeran song, "Castle on the Hill," an old favorite, and it's about driving, so it feels appropriate. Come on, Ed, sing me there safely.

It feels like I've been driving forever. My knuckles

are white on the wheel, and my whole body's starting to ache from the tension. This isn't like driving on back roads on a summer day. There's a delay between when I move the wheel and when the truck follows, like I'm steering a boat. But I'm so close I can see the halo of the streetlight above the diner. It's the finish line. I let out the breath I've been holding and hit the gas just a little harder. I don't see it until it's too late. It's a shadow in the dark, and then it's antlers and hooves, a deer ambling across the road—

I slam on the brakes and pull hard on the steering wheel.

The world goes spinning.

My head bangs against the window.

I cry out and cover my face from whatever comes next.

I can hear the engine ticking like a bomb. I look up, but everything's fuzzy and backward. I'm facing the wrong direction. I've spun off the street into the opposite ditch. I try the engine. It whirs but won't start. In the glare of the headlights, I can see the wobbly *S* my tires traced across the road. I can't find the deer. Maybe it made it? I hope so. Man, my head hurts. The radio's still playing.

What time is it? I've got to get to Mom. My head feels like a book someone's wedged too tight on the shelf. I can't get my seat belt off. My hands are shaking too badly. After a thousand years, or maybe a few seconds, I find the buckle and click it. That's when I see the blue lights flashing in the rearview mirror.

I wait.

And watch the cop grow larger in the mirror.

"Ma'am," he says, and raps the window with his knuckles. I jump. It's too loud in my ear, which is resting against the glass. The beam from his flashlight is too bright. There are two halos dancing instead of one. That can't be normal. He opens the door and I fall out. I'd forgotten about the seat belt.

"Ma'am?" he says again, this time like he's not sure, because now he sees I'm just a kid. "I'm Officer Ramos, and I'm here to help you. Can you tell me your name? How old you are? Where are your parents?" It's too many questions, and he's bent over me like a monster in a nightmare. Any second he's going to get too close. I can't make my mouth work. And then I hear her.

"Louise! Louise!"

I squint into the darkness and see Mom running toward me in her waitress uniform. Her hair's falling out of her ponytail. I cry out in relief.

"Mom. Your c-c-c-coat?" I'm shaking too hard to get it to come out right. The officer tries to give me his jacket, but I back up against the open door of the truck. He doesn't understand. She's the one that needs a coat. Not me. My head is pounding. Please don't let him touch me. He puts a hand out to stop Mom from getting any closer when she reaches us, and then he picks up a walkie-talkie attached to his shoulder. "Dispatch, I need an ambulance to the corner of Grove and Vista Place." He pauses and looks from me to Mom. "And call CPS. We need someone to meet us at the hospital."

"What's going on?" Mom is literally jumping in place. I want to tell her it's okay. I'm okay. We can still make it out in time. Why won't my mouth work?

"Ma'am, is this your daughter?"

"What? Yes. Yes, she's mine." She darts around him to get closer to me and puts a hand on my face. It's warm and I lean into it.

"I'm going to have to ask you to step away." Officer Ramos takes Mom by the shoulder, and she spins to face him like a cat, stiff and mean. Her hand is gone from my face too fast. I miss it.

"Don't you tell me to *step away* from my daughter. This is my baby girl."

I want to tell her to calm down. Not to make it worse. But there's a pulsing in my head that's thumping harder and harder. It's started to snow again.

"Ma'am, an ambulance is on the way. Your daughter's been in an accident. We all need to work together now to make sure she's okay." I can't see his face, but I get his tone. It's flat. He's already decided what kind of mother she is. I struggle to sit up. I hear sirens.

"It's not her fault," I say, but it's more a croak than actual words and not loud enough. "I was coming to pick her up."

He looks at me, eyebrows raised. "You were coming to pick her up?" Emphasis on "you."

"Honey, don't say anything else." Mom moves so she's between me and Officer Ramos. "We'll work this out."

"I need you to come with me, ma'am. We'll all be going down to the hospital together." He puts his hand out, offering to help her navigate the slippery snow. But she walks straight into it and glares at his fingers on her arm.

"Do not touch me." She's itching for a fight.

"Ma'am, you are clearly agitated." Now he moves so he's between the two of us. I can't even see her over his shoulder. No! "We're going to take care of your daughter, but you're going to have to calm down."

"Like hell I will." She's up in his face now, pushing at his chest and hitting at his shoulders.

"Mom, no! No!" I grab the truck door and pull up to stand.

The world sways. A spinning top. And me on top of it. I stumble forward and fall to my knees. And then there are hands on me that are not my mother's. I scream. The sirens scream. Everything flashes red, white, red, white. And then it fades to black.

3

Law and Order

"Can you tell me your name?" A woman leans over me with a penlight. It's too bright, like staring into the sun. I don't usually mind lights. But this is sudden and terrible. I flinch and turn my head, which makes the room spin. Her sleeve brushes up against my arm. I want her to go away.

"Louise Montgomery."

She shifts the light to the other eye and the world goes white. I blink and see spots. She's still too close. I feel trapped—pinned down like a bug.

"How old are you, Louise?"

"Twelve. I'm twelve. C-can you move your arm?"

"Sorry, honey. All done." She clicks off the light and straightens up. I scoot away from her and look around. I'm in a curtained-off room in a hospital. Maybe the ER? I hear lots of talking. A baby's crying somewhere, and somebody else is asking for water. Too many people. Too close. My arms start to itch, and I scratch at them under the blanket.

"Where's my mom?"

The doctor, Dr. Janson, her name tag reads, looks away, and I follow her eyes to someone I hadn't noticed sitting in a chair in the corner. It's a woman in a suit jacket and skirt. She looks like a lawyer-banker-school-librarian. She's holding a folder.

Dr. Janson doesn't answer my question. Instead, she looks back at me and says, "It looks like you've got a mild concussion from the accident. That's a nasty bump on your head. We'll need to keep you for observation. We're working on getting you a room up in pediatrics. But it might be a bit. It's a busy night with the snow." She pats my knee and I flinch. I see the woman in the suit see it. "Can I get you something to eat? Juice? Crackers?"

I shake my head. I can't spend the night here in this loud, too-bright place. I've never slept anywhere without my mom. I turn to the suited lady. "When can I see my mom?"

She stands and walks over. I get a better look at her. She's older than I thought, with silver running through her dark hair. I see a wedding ring. A nice old married lady has come to talk to me. This can't be good.

"That's what I'm here to see you about, Louise."

"Lou."

"Lou. You go by Lou. That's good. Thank you for telling me. My name is Maria, and I'm with the Placer County Child Protective Service. It's nice to meet you."

Well, it's not nice to meet you, I think.

CPS. This is exactly what we've been running from, and now they're here, the government, sitting in my hospital room, and my mom is off somewhere, maybe even in jail, and it's all my fault. I pinch my elbows under the covers until the tears that were about to fall shrivel back up, and I close my eyes. I play the game I used to play when I was little. If I can't see them, then they can't see me.

"Lou, you're old enough to understand the process, so I'll walk you through it, but you need to know you're not alone. You are safe here, and we will make sure you are well taken care of. Okay?"

I open my eyes. But I don't answer.

"Your mom is talking with the members of the hospital staff as well as the police officer, Officer Ramos, who found you on the scene."

On the scene. It sounds so criminal, when all I was trying to do was pick up my mother from work.

"We want to know why you were driving underage, why you were left alone, and why, according to our records, she hasn't enrolled you in any of the area schools."

I start to explain. "We've only been here a few months, and—" But Maria cuts me off.

"And why you are significantly underweight and your blood panel indicates iron levels low enough to border on anemia. Lou, we often see this in kids who live below the poverty line."

She says it like there's an actual line we just happened to trip over. I look at her calves sticking out below her sensible skirt. They are thick and strong. She's probably never had to worry about her next meal. She knows nothing about our lives. She doesn't know that Mom always gives me the thickest blanket, the extra scoop of peanut butter, the first turn in the camp showers.

I remember something from health class in fourth grade. "It's because I'm a vegetarian, the iron stuff, not because we're poor," I say. She just nods and writes something down. I don't think it's a get-out-of-jail-free card. My head is getting heavy like a water balloon, and the thoughts are sloshing around without settling. I lie back on the pillow and close my eyes again. This is not happening. She is not here. I am in my sleeping bag in the truck. We are going to LA. Mom will shake me awake any second.

"I'll give you some peace and quiet now," Maria whispers. "But I'll be right outside if you need me." I feel her stand to leave. "Get some rest, Lou. I'll see you in the morning."

"And then I'll see my mom," I say. She doesn't respond. When I look up, she's already gone.

The night is a weird mash-up of tiny bits of sleep and bad dreams. They move me at around three a.m. when a room finally opens up on the pediatric floor. There are sunshines on the floors and a picture of a cow jumping over the moon on my wall. The nurses come in every hour to aim a light at my eyes and ask me questions like what season comes after winter and can I touch the tips of my index fingers together. There's an ice machine just outside my room. I cringe every time I hear the whirring that comes right before the *thunk-thunk-thunk* of the ice. Something about that sound feels like a knife scraping across a bare plate. It's terrible. And exhausting. Who needs that much ice at 4:08, 4:36, 5:13 in the morning? I can't sleep anyway, without Mom. My head hurts too much to cry.

By the time the door swings open at seven a.m. and Dr. Janson comes in with Maria and a new nurse, I feel weak and shivery in a way that's worse than sitting in the snow with my head banged up.

"How are we feeling this morning?" Dr. Janson says with a hand on the bed rail, again too close to my hand.

"I'm okay." *Where's my mom?* I want to ask, but these people make me feel so small, I can't find any words that aren't answers to their questions.

"No dizziness? The nausea has gone away?"

I nod.

"Well, let's get you on your feet for a minute and check that balance. You've got a sizeable bump up there, and I want to make sure you're on the mend before we discharge you."

I slip out of the bed, feeling naked in the hospital gown. It's a child's size small but hangs off my bony shoulders and billows out in the back like a cape. The nurse reaches out a hand to steady me, but I dodge it and grip the bed rail. There've been way too many hands on me lately.

"Okay, Louise," Dr. Janson says. "Feet together and arms out to your sides. A little higher."

She reaches out and lifts my right wrist to shoulder height, but she does it with her pen, which is okay. I hold the position until my shoulders burn and arms shake. Which isn't very long.

"Okay, that's enough." She turns to the nurse. "I

42

think we're good to discharge tomorrow if the night goes well. That is"—she turns to Maria—"if you have everything you need from us in regards to placement?"

Maria nods. My stomach clenches. It's like a hunger pang, but I'm hollowed out by fear. What does she mean by "placement"? Are they trying to find a place for me and Mom to stay tonight? Did I total the truck? I climb back in bed and tuck my knees up under my chin. Maria and I watch the doctor and nurse leave.

"Is my mom outside?"

Maria pulls up a chair. She is in a different suit this time, a tan pantsuit with black stripes. She looks like someone from *Law & Order*.

"Lou. It's going to be a little bit before you see your mom."

My heart ticks twice and then stops. That can't be true. Mom would never let them get away with that. She's lying. She's trying to trick me into saying something that will get Mom in trouble.

"Why?" I say as calmly as I can. Underneath the sheets, my palms are clammy and cold.

"Our priority is you." Maria sets her folder on the

end of the bed near my left foot. I want to kick it. "We need to make sure you are safe and well cared for in your home environment."

"My mom did care for me, *does* care for me. You're the one keeping me out of my 'home environment.'" It comes out a little panicky. Why is she doing this to us?

Maria's shoulders slump in her shoulder pads. "Lou, you were living in your car, and it's about to be winter. That is not safe."

My heart kicks back in, but at double speed. I can't breathe. I can't stay here one more second! I rip off the sheets and jump down. I almost fall but catch myself.

"We were about to go to LA! Please, please let me see her," I beg. And then I start crying. I want my mom. A dark, deep pit has opened up in my stomach. I *need* my mom.

"Honey." Maria puts a hand on my shoulder. I howl like an animal and run to the opposite side of the room. I bang on the window and scream until my throat's raw and bitter tasting.

A nurse bursts in, and Maria holds out her hand like a traffic cop. "We're okay."

Eventually I stop screaming, mostly because it hurts too much. Maria has been standing still this whole time. She watches me crawl back into bed. I pull the blanket over my head and pretend, once again, that she is not there.

"Lou, I promise not to touch you again without your say-so, okay?"

Maria's voice has changed, there's a different kind of pity there. She understands now that I am not normal.

Good.

"For now, until we sort this out with your mother, we've found a relative with whom we can place you. A judge expedited the orders this morning. You were lucky. It can take up to a month in foster care before we would even get a hearing."

"Not my grandparents?" I say from under the sheet. Even though I know the answer. Mom hasn't spoken to them since I was born.

"Not your grandparents. It's your mom's sister, your aunt Ginger, and her husband."

"But . . ." I lift my head up. Aunt Ginger. I barely remember her. She's just a freckled face in a grassy field

45

under a summer sky. I haven't seen her in years. I don't even know where she lives.

Maria answers my unspoken question. "They're awaiting our arrival tomorrow night in Nashville."

"Why?"

"Why what?" Maria asks.

"Why'd the judge 'expedite' the order?" Maybe foster care wouldn't have been so bad. At least I could have been in the same state as Mom.

"Lou," Maria says, and something about her gentler tone makes my stomach drop. "Your mother requested it."

My mother. My mother is sending me away.

I cover my head and howl again, but only on the inside.

4

Leaving on a Jet Plane

I t's Friday. I stand in the hospital's tiny bathroom. There's a shower with a handicap bar, and the toilet has a red emergency cord dangling above it.

PULL IF YOU NEED ASSISTANCE.

I wonder what kind of assistance they mean. If I pull it, will someone get my mom? Get our truck? Get our life back? No one asked me what I wanted. I lock the door and consider never coming out.

It's been a good while since I looked at myself properly. I turn toward the mirror and take a deep breath and meet my own eyes. I am a ghost. I am the thing you imagine at your window at night. There are dark circles under my eyes, almost like pits, and I can't tell if that's because of the wreck or not sleeping or maybe this is how I always look. The bump on the left side of my head is a nasty knot, purple in the middle and yellow at the edges like a rotten sunflower.

One corner of my lip has split. There's a little dried blood there. And my hair needs washing. It usually does. It's stringy. The last time I had a decent shampoo was last Monday before the show at Joe's. Mom wanted me to look nice for "potential investors." We used the campsite showers, which are really just a box of stalls near the port-o-johns. I scratch at my head. The shower behind me is small, but beautifully clean. There's no mold in the corners or someone else's hair clogging the drain. It calls to me.

Underneath the hottest water I can stand, I rub the bar of soap into my scalp and under my arms and watch the dirt whirl away down the drain. There's so much of it. I wonder if they let Mom shower. Is she in a jail cell, like with actual bars and a metal toilet? Despite the heat I start to shake. I miss her so much it hurts. I sit down and let the water run over my head while I cry . . . again.

I'm toweling off when a knock on the door makes me jump.

"Lou, it's Maria. I'm leaving your clothes by the door." I hear her on the other side. I can see the shadow of her feet. But when I don't say anything, she eventually leaves. I wait another minute while the steam clears and then inch open the door. My sweatshirt and jeans are folded neatly on a chair. They've been washed, and there's a new pair of underwear and socks still in their packages. My boots and suede jacket sit underneath.

I feel a tiny bit better once I'm dressed in my own clothes. I fold up my used towel and nightgown and lay them at the end of the bed. Mom cleaned hotel rooms for a while. Even in the truck she likes us to be tidy. Then I sit and wait. There's a TV up in the corner, but I don't turn it on. I *need* to talk to Mom. Something about this whole thing doesn't add up. I *know* Mom. She'd fight tooth and nail for me. Somebody tricked her into sending me away. I know it. I pick up the white hospital phone, but after a minute of sitting and listening to the dial tone, I set it back down. I don't even have a number to call. *Mom, come get me,* I think, and curl up on the bed again.

Eventually the trio comes back in—Dr. Janson, Nurse Caroline, and Maria. Everyone's holding a pile of papers. Everyone looks fake cheery. It gives me the shivers.

"Looks like you're all clear, Louise," Dr. Janson says. "Here are your discharge papers. Remember, Tylenol or ibuprofen every four to six hours as long as the headaches persist. But if you're stilling having them in a week, you need to make an appointment with a primary care physician. And you'll need to do that in a month, regardless. Understand?"

Nurse Caroline hands me the papers. I take them. Nod. See, I am capable. *Let me go home.*

Maria opens her folder and hands me a ticket. I look at it for a full thirty seconds. It's a plane ticket from Reno to . . . *Los Angeles.* Something blooms in my chest—hope.

"So, I'm really going? With Mom?" Maybe they just had to make sure everything was on the up-and-up before they let us go. Maybe Mom's right outside. I take a step toward the door. "Mom and I are flying to LA?"

But Maria shakes her head. "We change planes in LA, Lou, on our way to Nashville."

Mom's not outside. Mom is nowhere I can get to. The spark of hope burns as it fizzles out.

"Your aunt wanted me to tell you how excited she is to have you," Maria is saying, but I'm not listening. I'm staring at the ticket that meant one thing just a second ago and now means something else entirely.

"I'm not going," I hear myself say. I've never said no to an adult in my life. It feels big—like earthquake, hurricane big. But Maria just sighs.

"Lou, you are still a minor. I understand you don't want to leave your mother, but at this time everyone feels that it's in your best interest to go to Tennessee."

Everyone. Surely she doesn't mean Mom, too? My face crumples. She sees it and starts to put a hand out but remembers her promise not to touch me and lets it fall.

"Honey, I know this is hard. And scary. But it is my entire job to make sure you are well cared for. I promise to keep you safe."

I *was* cared for. I *was* safe.

I pocket the ticket and scream really loudly in my head. No one wants to hear what I have to say. No one cares. Mom cared, or I thought she did. But Mom's not here. Maria waits by the bed while I gather my things—a plane ticket, a jacket, and Mom's guitar that she passed on to Maria to give to me. I don't want her guitar. I want *her*. I'm leaving without my mom, and there's nothing I can do about it.

The airport in Reno is jam-packed. I have never been to an airport before. I don't tell Maria this. She needs to think I can take of myself. *I* need to think I can take care of myself.

Maria explains that I won't be able to take the guitar with me on the plane. We have to "check it," whatever that means. When the man at the Southwest counter starts to take it from me, I can't let go. No one touches Mom's guitar but me and her. That's the rule. He looks confusedly from me to Maria.

"I promise they'll take good care of it," she says, gently pulling the case out of my hands without actually touching them. It slides away on a black conveyor belt, and I feel like a part of my soul is going with it.

Then we move to security. The line snakes back and forth, row after row of people who are too close together. Every time we make it around a corner, there's just more people. When a rolling suitcase bumps against my calf, I have to tug on my hair to keep myself from screaming.

When we finally get to the metal detector, I narrow my eyes at it, a too-small box that may or may not sound an alarm when I step into it. I step back.

"No."

Maria says, "Lou, this is standard procedure," as if that matters.

I shake my head so fast it whips my hair across my face and stings. Standard procedure.

"No."

The line builds up, and people start to file around us, like we're rocks in a river.

A guy in a security outfit with a name tag that reads JORGE asks me to step aside.

Maria follows and says, "She's with me. Child Protective Services." She shows him her ID.

"Miss, if you won't go through the metal detector, then we'll have to do a personal check," he says, and then before I can answer, he yells, "I need a female check over here!" I flinch.

A woman in the same blue security getup as Jorge walks up. She's snapping on gloves, and my stomach flip-flops. What does she plan to do with *those*?

"Hi, honey. I'm Sheela. I'm going to be performing your security check." I look at her through my curtain of hair. She sounds nice enough, but my eyes are on the gloves. If this is like the hospital, you don't put on gloves unless you plan to touch a person. I'm not going to let her touch me.

"Here's how it's going to go. I will ask you to lift your arms at your sides." She mimics lifting her arms at right angles to her body just like I had to do with Dr. Janson. "I'm going to use my hands"—she holds up her gloved hands like a magician—"and run them along your back, down your sides, and rib cage, right here." She touches her own waist and runs her hands up under her armpits. I take a step back. No. No way am I letting her do that to me.

"Lou," Maria says. "It's this"—she points at Sheela—"or that"—she points at the giant black box. "If you refuse, we can't fly."

"Good."

I watch her exhale slowly through her nose and smooth the black and gray strands that have escaped from her bun. She leans down then, so we are eye to eye. "Lou, do you understand that if I can't get you to Nashville to stay with your aunt and uncle, you will be placed in the temporary custody of a foster family?"

I picture this—people I don't know telling me how to dress and what to eat and where to go. It's not like Aunt Ginger is any different. But at least I can kind of remember her face. She and Mom have the same eyes, I think. I close my eyes and try to swallow. I spread my arms and pretend this is all in my head. For a second there's nothing but the sound of airport announcements and the whirring of the conveyor belt pumping out carry-ons. I begin to hum the only song I can think of—"You Are My Sunshine"—to have a familiar sound in my head.

Then Sheela's hands are on my back. I stop humming

and grind my teeth. Her hands travel up my back and under my arms. I bite down so hard my jaw aches. And then she moves her hands down to my waist, and I can't take it anymore. I smack at her hands and run a few feet away, against the benches where the people who are pulling on their shoes stop to watch me. Jorge follows. He looks nervous. I don't care. I don't care if I live with a foster family. I'll just run away back to Mom, wherever she is. I will *not* let Sheela touch me again.

Maria pulls Sheela aside and whispers something to her. Flashes her ID again. They talk a minute longer while Jorge and I watch. Something in Sheela's face softens, and then they both nod.

"All right, honey," Sheela says as she walks back up to me over by the benches. She holds up a black wand-looking thing. "I'm just going to wave this down your back and up your front. No touching, okay?"

I look to Maria and she nods.

"Okay," I whisper.

When we get to the gate, I collapse into a puddle in one of the seats. I have that total boneless feeling I get when a performance is over. Except this isn't over. I've only made it through security. I've still got to actually get on a plane and fly across the country. I can see the plane from here, like a giant silver bullet with wings. I've never asked Mom if she's flown. Will this be something I do that she's never done? For the millionth time today, I wish I could talk to her.

Maria sits down next to me with two chicken burritos from the neon-lit food court. I eat mine so fast I swallow a little of the foil wrapping, too. I picture Mom laughing and shaking her head. She'd pass me a napkin and say, *Manners, Lou. We're not* animals.

When we board, Maria makes sure I'm on the aisle so I don't feel cramped. We sit in the first row. I study the plastic emergency pamphlet. All the cartoon people look weirdly calm while they barrel down an inflatable slide into the ocean. My heart hiccups. I put the pamphlet away and rub my sweaty hands on my knees.

The plane jerks, and I grip my armrests as we pull away from the gate. This can't be normal? I lean into the aisle and look behind me. People are already asleep or watching movies. When I turn back around, the flight attendant smiles and mouths, *It'll be okay*, and then picks up a phone on the wall to explain how to put on your oxygen mask. I feel a little bump on the runway and tighten my seat belt.

And then the craziest thing happens. The flight attendant breaks into song. Right there in front of me as we rumble down the runway, she starts to sing "Leaving on a Jet Plane" at full volume into the inter-com. I stare at her with my mouth open, and Maria smiles. She's got a good voice. A little showtuney, but strong. And I know this song. It's John Denver. I used to perform it before Mom decided it was too slow. It's not slow how this lady's doing it, though.

I close my eyes and smile. For a second I forget where I am and see us, Mom and me, at a farmer's mar-ket in Oklahoma. I'm singing this song and it's July and muggy hot, but the tips are piling up and the audience is easy and when it's done, Mom scores us free fresh-squeezed lemonade, and it's the coldest, sweetest thing I've ever had.

Then the plane jerks so hard I'm thrown back in my

seat, and there's a sound like a roaring animal. It shakes the whole plane, and I look down at my armrest swaying like my seat is attached to nothing at all. We're crashing. I'm drowning in the noise and blinded in a wave of white panic. I try to cover my ears, but the sound creeps in around the edges. I taste the burrito coming up hot and chunky at the back of my throat. The roaring isn't stopping. It's never going to stop! I dig my nails into my scalp and pull hard at the roots. I stomp my feet over and over until they tingle. Somewhere, someone is screaming. It's me.

I cry for one hour and sixteen minutes—the entire length of the flight to Los Angeles. The passengers across the aisle request to move. A little kid in a Lakers cap asks his mom, "What's wrong with her?" on the way to the bathroom. Maria keeps passing me tissues and making me sip water. But she's no help. The flight attendant looks like she's ten years older by the time we land.

"Okay, listen." Maria kneels in front of me with her beige knees on the dirty floor of the terminal. My hair is dripping around the edges from the water I splashed on my face in the bathroom. "We need a game plan."

"I can't do it." I don't cry. There's nothing left but a wet hiccup. People are rushing past us, dragging kids and rolling bags. They all look so certain of where they're going.

"Yes. You can. You are stronger than you think." She says it with such sureness. The kind of sure you can only be when you barely know someone. "Tell me what triggered it. You looked all right just before take-off."

"I was okay when she was singing. But then the engines were so loud, I . . ." I can't finish it. I can't even think about it again.

Maria snaps her fingers and I jump. Everything's making me jump today. "That's it. The music. We need something loud enough to drown out the noise." She stands and looks around and then leads me to a gift shop selling metal water bottles that cost fifty dollars and chocolate truffles with the Hollywood Hills on them. Is this what LA is like? Could Mom and I have even afforded *water* in this city? Did Mom know what she was getting us into? It's still Friday. Today, a man named Howie and his wife will wait for a girl named Lou who will never show up. And then they will forget she ever existed.

"Okay," Maria says, coming out of the shop and crooking her finger. "You follow me." We wind our way through the terminal until we end up at a little vending machine. I expect to see Fritos and Snickers. But instead it's filled with black boxes. She swipes her credit card and hits F-10.

We stand side by side and watch a black box make its way across and down and out into Maria's waiting hand.

"Here."

"What is it?"

"Open it."

I peel off the clear sticker and open the box. Inside is a tiny iPod and headphones. I look up at her and then back at the most expensive vending machine I have ever seen.

"I can't afford this."

"Consider it a loan."

"But—"

"No 'buts.' We don't have a lot of time before our next flight. Let's get you set up."

We spend the next thirty minutes creating an Apple Music account on Maria's laptop and downloading Pink and Katy Perry and, yes, Dolly Parton, to get me through the four-hour flight to Nashville. I hope it's enough.

This time, before the flight attendant can even begin the safety talk, I put in my earbuds, hit play, turn the volume all the way up, and let the good noise out-shout the bad. I keep my eyes closed the whole time. By the time we land in Nashville, it is three o'clock in the morning and my head is throbbing and I still have to meet my mysterious aunt Ginger and I am now farther away from Mom than I have ever been. But I did it. I flew across the country, and I did not fall apart. Not all the way, anyway.

5
Music City, USA

I slip the iPod in my jacket pocket and then pat it and keep patting it all the way down the long empty terminal. With no people to dodge, it feels bigger and calmer, like walking the mall after closing time. All of a sudden I kind of like airports.

Maria had requested that Aunt Ginger and her husband, Dan, wait for us in baggage claim. She stops me just before the escalator. We are standing under a big cutout of a guitar that makes me wish I had Mom's in my hands. She kneels again in her suit, now wrinkled and grimy at the cuffs from a morning at a hospital and the rest of a day on planes. Sixty percent of her hair has escaped its bun, and she kind of looks like a mad scientist, but when she smiles, her eyes crinkle like Mrs. Claus.

"Got your iPod?"

I pat my pocket again. I'm worried now about the big meetup and also so tired I could curl up under this fake guitar and sleep for a week. Maria's already told me this is where we part ways. She'll be staying until tomorrow to confer with my new caseworker, whatever that means, and whoever that is, and then she'll fly back to Tahoe. I hope she fights for Mom, too, even though she keeps saying, "You're my first concern, Lou." It's a little scary that as of right now, Maria is the person who knows me the most in the whole wide world, outside of Mom. The people downstairs are strangers. I don't want her to leave.

"Now I want you to listen to me very carefully before we say good-bye." She doesn't try to take my hand, but she does lean in, and I'm looking at the top of her graying head and then finally meeting her eyes. "I know these people are new. This town is new. And maybe it will only be for a little while. If what you tell me about your mother is true, then I hope so. But this is an opportunity, Lou. No. Don't roll your eyes at me. It is. I meant it when I said you are tough. I know the world can be too loud sometimes and too close—"

I let my eyes slide off hers and back down to my feet.

"But you are not the only one who feels like that. Look at me."

I do.

"You are not the only one scared of noise or crowds or planes or strangers and the unknown. I've seen your file from the school in Biloxi. I know you've had a hard run. But I also know you're smart. And this is a chance to find out more about yourself and to learn who you are when everything else falls away. This is an *opportunity*."

I'm so tired of hearing how I have to fight for everything. For someone who won't let me see Mom, Maria sounds a lot like her. It makes me want to hold on to her sleeve.

"There's more than just an iPod to get you through,

Louise. But you've got to be curious. You promise to do that? To be curious?"

I nod. Because what choice do I have?

She gets up. "All right, then. Let's go."

Maria walks onto the escalator, and I let one, two, three steps go by and then follow. Over the loudspeaker, Johnny Cash is singing "Ring of Fire," and I think, *Yeah, that's sounds about right.*

The baggage carousel has already stopped. I spot Mom's battered guitar case covered in stickers before I notice the woman with the bright red hair holding it in her arms. She's holding it all wrong, cradling it like a baby. She shouldn't be touching it at all. Who gave her the right? Next to her is a very tall, very blond guy.

Maria walks up first and holds out a hand, but it's not to shake. She's asking for ID. "Mr. and Mrs. Latimer?"

"Yes, I'm Mrs. Latimer, Ginger, and this is Daniel."

Daniel fumbles with his driver's license after Maria hands it back. Then he turns to me. "You must be Louise. Ginger's told me so much about you." He holds his hand out, but I stick my fists in my pockets and fiddle with the iPod. How does Ginger know anything about me to tell?

"Hi, Lou," Ginger says, and offers up Mom's guitar case to me. I was right. She has hazel eyes, same as Mom, same as me.

"Hi," I mumble, and hold the case by the handle, as it was meant to be held.

Silence trips over us like we're a crack in the sidewalk. Then Maria breaks the quiet. She's all business.

"Mrs. Latimer, Louise's caseworker, Melissa, will be by tomorrow afternoon after we meet to discuss the current custody status. For now, as the closest living relative and appointed guardian in case of an emergency, you have been granted temporary placement. Obviously, we will keep you apprised as the situation unfolds."

As the situation unfolds . . . like it's a Christmas present and not the unraveling of my whole life. I don't want to go with these people. I don't want to be in this airport at ridiculous o'clock in the morning. We walk together as a group toward the exit, but then Maria starts to turn left at the line for shuttles while Ginger and Dan head for the parking lot.

"Wait!" I yelp, and everybody freezes.

"Maria, please tell my mom . . ." And then I can't think what to say. There are too many things. *Remember to eat. Don't smoke all day just because I'm not there to stop you. Don't pick fights with the people trying to help. I've got your guitar. I'll keep it safe. We'll reschedule with the Mazes. Come get me.* Finally, I choke out, "Tell her I love her."

Maria smiles and wipes at her eyes once and says, "I will, Lou. I promise." Then she walks out, and I am following two people I wouldn't recognize in a crowd into the parking lot. And then we stop. It's a sea of cars, and Ginger holds out her keys and points them at it. And then she begins to point them in every direction.

"I'm sorry," she says, and we start to walk down the rows. "We were just so distracted getting here, and it was so late." She pauses and cuts through the middle of a row. Dan steps back and waits for me to follow her before taking his place behind me. I feel hemmed in. "I can't remember for the life of me . . . ," she says, and then we see a flash of lights off to our right. She cheers. I jump back and step on Dan's toe. He doesn't seem to notice as we follow Ginger to a white SUV. It's a Lexus. My mother's sister drives a big shiny *Lexus*. Dan sees my mouth fall open and kind of shrugs. I slide onto the leather backseat without a word. There's only so much a person can process in one day without losing the power of speech.

I rest my hand on the guitar next to me and watch the landscape slip along the highway and try not to think about how *this* woman, who's talking nonstop from behind the wheel, came to be my mom's emergency contact and why I haven't see her since I was a kid.

6
Castaway

The room I wake up in is blue, very pale blue with white wooden shutters and carpet so thick and soft it feels like walking on fur. I scooch up under the covers and make a nest of pillows on the queen-size bed. I am a bird in an egg.

The clock on the table next to me says it's one o'clock . . . in the afternoon. We didn't get here until almost five in the morning. The sun was just beginning to rise. Guilt rattles around in my head at the thought that I slept so hard in a nice fluffy bed while Mom is who knows where. I have to count the days in my head to figure out it's Saturday now. I can hear a radio or television going somewhere in the distance. This house is big enough to have a "somewhere in the distance." And I smell bacon and something else . . . blueberry muffins, maybe? My stomach gives a grumpy gurgle. It wants its breakfast. One day of real meals and it's already high maintenance.

I look around my new bedroom. It has a couch that Ginger named the "reading chair," under the window-sill. I have my own bathroom. And a white desk with a little lamp on it. A fan turns slowly above me. I feel turned inside out.

I get up and brush my teeth with a brand-new tooth-brush and toothpaste that tastes like bubblegum and then walk out onto "the landing." That's what Ginger called it. It's really just the top of the stairs that overlooks the living room, which has wood floors and a fireplace and glass doors like the ones at Joe's that open out onto a stone patio with a fire pit, because apparently, Dan likes to invite his book club over, and that's where they meet. Dan is an English teacher at the middle school I'll be going to and also the tennis coach, which makes sense when I think of his long pale limbs. I can just see him in white knee socks swinging a racket.

I know all this because Ginger talked *a lot* on the car ride home. She talked until I actually fell asleep standing in the doorway to my new room. But now I'm not so tired. And this new place is . . . scary. The carpet is too soft and thick and it makes all the other sounds in the house too quiet, like they're being smothered. My room is too bright and alien compared to our cozy truck. I miss my red sleeping bag. I miss hearing the sound of the waves lapping on the shore of the lake. I even miss Mom's smoky smell.

I creep downstairs, thinking maybe I'll step outside for a minute to catch my breath, but then I hear someone banging around in the kitchen. It's too loud. I shake my head, take a step back, and bump into Dan. I bite the inside of my cheek. How can this house be so big and so *crowded* at the same time?

He smiles sheepishly. "Hey there," he says, folding a half-marked-up crossword puzzle under his arm. He was coming out of "the study," which is basically a room lined floor to ceiling with books. He's in a plaid button-down and jeans and moccasins. He looks like an L.L. Bean advertisement.

"Hey."

"You hungry? Ginger decided she's Martha Stewart today, so we're finally using all the pots and pans we got for our wedding, five years later."

I tuck my hands inside the sleeves of my sweatshirt and stare at my feet. I wonder if Mom even knows Ginger is married. She must if she had a number to put on her emergency contact sheet.

"You know, we could, uh, wash those for you." He points at my clothes. "Or take you shopping if you don't like what Ginger picked out."

"Uh, maybe later."

I refuse to change into the leggings and black sweater Ginger set out for me on my dresser, no matter how soft they are. This sweatshirt and jeans are the last things I have from home. It's what I was wearing the last time I saw Mom.

"Breakfast! Or lunch or brunch or whatever it is!" Ginger calls from the kitchen, and I'm glad for the escape.

The big wooden table in the kitchen seats eight, and there are already places set for us with a vase of pansies in the middle. It's so formal, I'm afraid I'm going to break something. I miss Mom's Styrofoam boxes of cold hash browns with a dash of Tabasco, just the way I like them.

I wait until they both sit so I know where to go. In front of us are steaming plates of eggs and bacon and blueberry muffins. I consider not eating, out of solidarity with Mom, but my stomach growls so loud it sounds like a dog under the table.

"Oh, wait!" Ginger jumps up as I'm unfolding my napkin. "I forgot the juice!" She seems frazzled, or maybe this is how she always is. I study her as she walks toward the kitchen island. I know she's three years older than Mom, but she looks so much younger. Her hair is more orangey than red in this light. I think it's natural. And there're no lines around her eyes.

I start to take a forkful of eggs, but then I hear it. *Whir-whir-buzzzzzzz. Whir-whir-clink!* It's the blender. I drop my fork on the floor, spilling goopy eggs all over the nice rug. I grab my napkin and duck down to try to clean it, but the blender is still going and I have to stop and plug my ears. It goes on and on and on, and I am still under the table. I see Dan's knee bouncing in his chair, but he doesn't lean down and look at me. I want to cry. It's embarrassing, but it also *hurts*. That's what nobody gets. The sounds actually hurt, like knives someone is throwing at me.

And then it stops. Very slowly, I get up and sit back down. My face is hot, and I can tell Dan's watching me but pretending not to. Please don't let me have ruined their rug. Ginger comes in without a clue and hands me a glass of blood-red juice.

"Fresh tomato juice! Full of vitamins!"

Clumps of seeds and pulpy chunks are floating on the top like algae on a pond. I want to crawl back under the table. She waits until I take a teeny-tiny sip before she sits.

We eat mostly in silence. I push my juice to the farthest corner of my place mat. Dan tries to talk to me about Chickering Academy, the middle school I'll be starting, but I don't want to think about that yet. I'm still hoping all of this will be over before Monday.

I hear a bump and then another, and the dishes on the table rattle. I can't figure out where it's coming from until Ginger says, "Dan," in that voice you use to wake someone up from a bad dream.

"What? Oh sorry, I'll stop."

Apparently, Dan's knee-bouncing is a regular thing. Mom used to hate it when I jiggled my legs on long drives. She said being still was a skill. But the wiggling was (and still is) soothing, like letting out little flares of nervous energy. I study Dan across the table. He's all elbows and glasses and ears. He's exactly like a kid with too much energy. I wonder if I'm supposed to call him "Uncle" Dan. I hope not.

The big wooden clock in the hall chimes twice, and Ginger stands up to take my dishes. I'm reminded that most people don't always eat off plates you throw away.

"Your new caseworker will be here in an hour. Want me to run you a bath?" she asks.

"No, thank you." It's weird having someone cook for me and lay out clothes and try to talk to me about school. That's not how Mom and I function. We're a team, but we know how to take care of ourselves.

I shower in my new bathroom and put the old Hard Rock Cafe sweatshirt back on. That's two showers in two days. A record. Then I sit on the big white bed and hold Mom's guitar. I don't play it—just close my eyes and let my fingers feel the strings, the back of the neck, the upper frets. I sing an old Willie Nelson song that was one of Mom's favorites to pass the time and calm my mind.

When the doorbell rings a half hour later, it's a symphony of bells. I walk out onto the landing and peek down at the top of Ginger's and Dan's heads. They give each other a look like they're starting a relay race, and Dan tugs on the end of Ginger's ponytail before she opens the door. Mom never dated, not really. I've never lived with two grown-ups under one roof.

Ginger is saying, "Please, please come in," and I sneak forward to get a better look. Dan spots me and waves me down. If having two adults around means two sets of eyes, maybe it's not all it's cracked up to be. I shake my head and take a step backward toward my room, but then Ginger turns now too and waves at me.

"Lou, come on down and meet Melissa!" she says in this weird high-pitched voice I haven't heard her use yet.

I tuck my hands into my sleeves and shuffle down the stairs as slowly as possible. If Mom were here, she'd tell me to "stop draggin' your feet" and "walk like you've got places to *go*," but I don't think she meant places like this.

Melissa, my new caseworker, is not what I expected. She has a pixie haircut and earrings that run up and down both ears. There's one in her nose, too. She's also wearing all black. I see a motorcycle in the driveway behind her. Melissa is cool. Maybe she'll get where Mom and I are coming from.

She walks straight past Dan and Ginger and makes a beeline for me. I back up against the stair post.

"Hi. You must be Lou." She cocks her head at me. "Maria's talked you up."

I swallow and nod. What am I supposed to say?

"Why don't we all go in the living room?" Dan suggests, because Ginger doesn't seem to know what to do with herself. She keeps smoothing down her sweater.

"I'd like to see Lou's room first," Melissa says, all

business, like Maria. Ginger points up the stairs, and we all take our places to follow Melissa like kids. She sticks her head in the blue room. "Nice digs." And then she spots the guitar on the bed and asks, "You play?"

"A little. It's my mom's."

"Well, you're in the right place if you want to learn. This is the music capital of the world."

She turns to Ginger and Dan and says without a pause, "No kids, Mr. and Mrs. Latimer?"

"What? Oh, no. Not yet." Ginger puts a hand to her ponytail. "We thought we'd enjoy married life a bit first. I mean, not that kids aren't *wonderful* . . ." She trails off and looks horrified that she just implied she didn't want kids running around her nice house. She's got nothing to worry about. I don't want to be here either. But the thought that I'm in the way pinches a little.

Melissa raises her eyebrows but carries on. "Right, well, let's go back downstairs and have a chat." We follow her and sit on the brown leather couches around the empty fireplace.

"When can I see my mom?" I haven't asked the question in more than twelve hours. It feels like if I don't, she'll start to fade away. I need someone to tell me something that *matters*.

Melissa looks up from where she's laying out several folders on the coffee table and smiles. "I guess we'll get to it, then."

She folds her hands in her lap and leans back. "This is just an initial home inspection, to make sure you're comfortable and have everything you need. Now . . ." She pauses and gives me one of those up-and-down looks. "You want me to shoot you straight?" I nod. Ginger and Dan scoot closer together on the couch, making it squeak. "Your mom is currently under investigation for child neglect." I start to open my mouth. Melissa presses on. "I know. I know. It was a complicated situation. You were parked at a campsite. She couldn't get to and from work without transportation. And she needed to work to keep you fed. But she should never have relied on a minor to pick her up in the middle of the night, especially in those conditions. And you should have been in school instead of singing on street corners."

Laid out like that, it sounds worse than when

Maria said it. I feel my head getting lighter and lighter, like it might just float away. I wish it would. I reach back and tug at the ends of my hair just once, hard, to keep myself from crying.

Ginger leans forward and puts her elbows on her knees. "My sister is a lot of things, but neglectful of her child is not one of them." She points at me. "She loves this girl. She has from the moment she was born, and I know she'd do anything to protect her." Something in her voice has shifted. It's steadier and louder. "Under California law, you can't keep her over seventy-two hours without formal charges. It's been three days. Have you charged her?"

Maybe's there's more to Ginger than a Lexus and lumpy tomato juice.

"As the investigation is still ongoing, Ms. Montgomery is required to remain in Tahoe City until both the police and social services have closed their cases. But she's not being held anywhere. She is free to work and go about her business. In fact, we encourage it. She needs a steady job, a home—evidence that she can provide a stable environment."

So Mom is okay. I let out a little sigh of relief. But then . . . why hasn't she called? And how is she going to get a *home* when she can't even afford the gas to LA without working double shifts?

"Everything looks good here for now," Melissa continues. "I'll be in touch at the end of the week once Lou gets settled in at . . ." She looks down at her papers and then raises her eyebrows. "Chickering Academy. Swanky." And then she's standing, and I'm still not any closer to seeing Mom. Things have gone off the rails. As if they weren't already.

Melissa shakes hands with Dan and Ginger, and then winks at me. I bet Maria put a note in my file about what happened at the airport. I bet there's a big *Do Not Touch!* warning all over those pages. Fine, let her get all the dirt she wants on me. Just give me my mom back!

"Good luck at school, Lou," she says, and gives me her card. "Call me if you need me. You're going to be all right. I will see to that. You hear me?"

"I hear you," I say, and I do. But it doesn't mean anything. Everybody says I'm going to be fine, but they just keep trading me off from person to person. She doesn't care any more than Maria did. They all leave and forget about me.

"Good," she says, and, no surprise, leaves. I watch her ride away on her motorcycle.

I run upstairs so I don't have to say another single thing to another person. I throw myself on the bed. It's so soft. I hate it. I mean, I hate that I like it. There are so many things I should have told Melissa. So far she only knows Mom as the woman who lets her daughter drive a pickup truck in the snow in the middle of the night and doesn't make her go to school, but *does* make her sing in front of strangers. There's so much more, though! Like when I was ten and dying to see the Country Music Awards. We were camping just outside Oklahoma City and didn't have a TV. But she made friends with the family in the fancy RV next door, and we got to watch the show on their plasma screen. We sat on their couch in that RV and analyzed Carrie Underwood's new guitar and Kacey Musgraves's orange pantsuit. We watched all the way until the end. I'd never been so tired and happy in my life.

I sigh and roll over, catching sight of Mom's guitar by the door. It's like having a piece of her here, which is great, but not enough. It's not nearly enough. Why did she send me here?

There's a knock, and Ginger peeks her head in. "Dan has tennis with the team this afternoon. Want to go for a walk?"

"Uh, sure." I really don't, but it's either that or stare at the guitar.

We leave Dan on the bottom step pulling on his very white tennis shoes and head into the late September sunshine. They live on a quiet street that backs up to a thicket of trees. At its edge there is a little wooden gate, like the kind you'd find in *The Secret Garden*. Ginger leads me through it. We leave the sunshine behind and wind our way under a canopy of maples and pines. It's quiet as we walk, just the *crunch crunch* of red and yellow leaves under our shoes. It's funny the sounds my body finds calming and the ones it doesn't. What glitch in my brain decided crunchy leaves are good and blenders and airplanes are bad?

"I like it here, away from the sound of traffic and

people," Ginger says like she's reading my mind. After a few minutes we stop at a footbridge that runs over a little creek. She leans on the railing and rubs her head like it hurts and then lets down her ponytail.

I ask the question that I've been wondering about since Melissa left. "How'd you know that stuff about California law?"

For a second Ginger looks confused, then surprised. "Didn't your mom tell you I'm a lawyer? I work in estate law, but I know enough about custody cases to ask the right questions." She looks at me a beat longer. "She didn't tell you anything about me, did she?"

"What's estate law?" I ask instead of admitting that *no, my mom has hardly mentioned you in my entire life.*

Ginger isn't fooled, but she answers anyway. "Estate law is managing other people's assets—houses, property, businesses. It's your net worth. Whatever you can rightfully call yours."

I think about my net worth. Borrowed guitar. Donated iPod. Clothes on my back. Imagine having enough that you'd need someone to keep track of it for you. I pick a yellow leaf off the rail of the bridge and tear it into tiny pieces. "Do you talk to my grandparents?"

She laughs, but she doesn't sound happy. "No. They weren't exactly thrilled when I got a scholarship to college, or what they called . . . and I quote . . . 'that highfalutin place.' They felt like I chose school over them."

"That's nuts."

She laughs again. "Yes, nuts is a good word for it. Lou, your grandparents are proud people. But they're proud about the wrong things. They wanted us both in our rightful places, whatever they decided those were."

"It doesn't make sense." I shake my head.

Ginger picks up her own leaf to shred. "I was a sophomore at the state college back in Arkansas when your mom told me she was going to have you. But she didn't tell our parents until *after* she dropped out of her senior year of high school. It was a sticky situation. Next thing I knew, she sent me a postcard from Little Rock saying she'd left home."

"Did you know my dad?"

This is a sneaky question, and I know it, because Mom has never answered this one either in the handful of times I've bugged her about it. But this is already more information than I've had on my family in twelve years, and I'm greedy for it. If Ginger's willing to talk, I'm going to ask.

She sighs. "Did you know I was named after Ginger on *Gilligan's Island*? Mama used to call me the red-haired starlet. But your mom, *she* was the knockout of the family, with that blond hair down to her waist and legs for miles. By the time she turned fifteen, the boys were lined up." She looks at me sideways. "She always told me she wasn't sure who your daddy was, and she didn't want to be sure either."

I already knew about the long line of boys and the fact that my dad could have been any one of them. But I had secretly hoped Mom might have said that to protect me, and really she knew. I hoped Ginger would know, that Mom had confessed it to her, and now I'd get my big reveal. There are too many big black holes in my life, and I'm starting to see it's because Mom chose to keep it that way. I don't get it. I don't get why everything has to be so hard.

I glance at Ginger. She's staring into the water, and

her hair's blowing a little in the breeze. She looks different after her talk with Melissa. Like she's found her regular setting and isn't so jumpy around me. And if she's anything like Mom, I bet she knows more than she's letting on.

"Do you still have that postcard from Little Rock?"

"Oh sure. And a few from Memphis and Lexington that your mom sent before you all moved west." She straightens up. "Want to see them sometime?"

That surprises me. She's actually going to let me see them. Mom would have hidden them or burned them on sight. She isn't one for mementos or anything that makes you remember, really.

"Yeah. Yeah, I do."

As we make our way back out of the trees and into the backyard, I do the math I always have to do when I count through all the places we've lived. I was only five when we left Lexington. Why did Mom stop writing after? Why send all those postcards before that and then just . . . nothing? Why didn't we visit? If she wanted me to "make it big," why not come to the music capital of the world? It doesn't make sense. None of this makes sense.

I slip off my shoes at the back door and say bye to Ginger before going upstairs. *Gilligan's Island* was that show about the people who got shipwrecked on an island. There were always old reruns in the motels where we stayed. Their little boat ride was only supposed to be a three-hour trip before the storm sent them spinning. Then they were castaways. Away from home for years and years.

7

Get Well Soon

I am on an island. I am on an island floating in a sea. It's not hard to imagine in this blue sea of a room with the light streaming through the lacy curtains like reflected waves. My mother is free, but she hasn't called. I keep circling back to that. Is she not allowed to? Is that it? Some rule Melissa didn't mention? Or am I the castaway now? I remember how Ginger described Mom's wild teenage self. It makes sense when I think of her like that. And now she's finally gotten the chance to cut loose from the thing that got her caught up all those years ago at seventeen. Me. I squeeze my eyes shut, but still a tear leaks out. It hurts. It hurts like sounds hurt. Like a physical punch.

But a memory floats to the surface, one late summer afternoon in Tahoe. We'd just finished a show for the lunch crowd down by the pier. It was a small group, thankfully, and I was proud of myself for keeping it together all the way to the end.

When we got back to the truck and I unlatched the guitar case to count our tips, I found a yellow piece of paper along with the usual coins and bills. It was a coupon for the fancy ice cream parlor.

Mom held up "lunch," a jar of peanut butter and a box of Ritz, and said, "No spoons, baby Lou. Hope your hands are cleanish."

I held up the coupon. "Ice cream places have spoons."

She sighed. You could buy a gallon tub at Kroger's for the price of one tiny scoop at this place. But she slipped it in her back pocket and took my hand.

As we walked back up the hill toward town, we hummed a little "You Are My Sunshine." Mom's always good with the harmony.

"Baby, you have the voice of an angel."

"So you say."

"You do, love. That's why I do this, you know. All this." She pulled me to a stop outside the warm glow of the Snow Cap Creamery, but I didn't want to hear that speech just then. Didn't want to be called her "better half" like she always did when I complained about the performing. I just wanted some ice cream. I took the coupon and walked in.

It was deliciously cool and quiet inside, and there was only one guy ahead of us in line. I took my time wandering in front of the cold case, eyeing the sherbet and the chocolate praline and the blueberry. We never got ice cream. Frozen food in a truck with nothing but a small cooler isn't exactly practical. Mom laughed as I paced in front of the counter, waiting for the guy in front to hurry up and pay already.

And then it happened.

He must have ordered a shake or smoothie or something, because the blender whirred to life like a demon, like Ginger's, but worse because it was only two feet away. I covered my ears, but the whining drone of it snuck past, and I began to shake, first my head and then my whole body. The girl in the striped apron at the blender had no idea. She kept going. A thousand bees in my head. My heart in my throat. I dropped the coupon and ran.

Mom found me crying on the sidewalk behind the Snow Cap five minutes later. Without a word, she handed me a double scoop of mint chocolate chip. My favorite. And then she hummed some more "You Are My Sunshine" while I ate. There was only one coupon. She didn't get a cone of her own.

I stare up at my ceiling. Mom would never abandon me. Never. Which leaves only one conclusion: This is all my fault. She's "under investigation" because I can't do a simple thing like drive a truck *two miles* down the road without wrecking our whole lives. Guilt twirls in my stomach like an eel, dark and slick. I taste the acidy tomato juice again and sit up. I will take this "opportunity," as Maria called it, to practice being normal here. So that by the time Mom calls me, I'll be her good-luck charm like always. We'll pick up with LA just like we planned.

Meanwhile, this is the day that *will not end*. The Saturday that stopped time. I hear a door slam downstairs. Dan's probably back from tennis. Nice, teachery Dan, who might very well be my English teacher on Monday. I put my earbuds in and crank the music up loud, dragging a pillow over my face to keep away any unwanted noises.

Not a minute later I feel a thwack, thwack, thwack at the foot of the bed and jerk upright. I yank out the earbuds. There is a boy in my room—a very skinny boy with dark hair and blue fingernails. And he is swinging a racket one inch from my foot.

"Well?" he says.

I hug my pillow. And then I try to speak. But my voice is hiding somewhere under the pillow next to my hammering heart.

"Well." He holds out a hand. At the threat of a handshake, I scoot back and knock into the headboard. It shakes loose my voice.

"Well what?" It's squeaky, but it's there.

"No. *Well.*" He points at himself with his racket. "I'm Well. You must be Louise."

His green T-shirt has a screen print of U2's *War* album on it, and it looks intentionally distressed. There is a red sweatband around his head like he's an extra in a Jazzercise video. It makes me curious and a teensy bit less nervous.

"Your name is Well?"

He sits down at the end of the bed. "Maxwell, actually, but that's atrocious. Nobody needs that kind of name unless they own a country. Am I right?"

I shrug. I'm still not sure what's happening right now. Well keeps talking.

"So, Coach Latimer said you were starting at Chickering on Monday. Listen, Lou. It's Lou, right? Listen, Lou, don't let them push you into dance or choir or whatever watercolor lily pad nonsense they're painting in art. You're taking theater. I'm in theater." He leans in and points his racket at me. "*Theater.* Promise me."

He's bossy. And acts like he already knows me. "I—I thought I'd just take English and math and science and . . . the normal stuff." As soon as I've said it, I wonder, *Is that the normal stuff?* I haven't been in school in more than a year. And it was elementary. I want Well to go away before he laughs at me.

And then he laughs at me.

"Ha, yeah, that's because you're normal. And that's what normal people expect. But this is *Chickering Academy*." He stops here and twirls his racket. "At Chickering," he says in a voice that sounds like the flight attendant giving announcements, "we like our pupils to be well-rounded, multitalented individuals." He leans in again. "Aka, you either play a sport or you join the arts."

He *wasn't* laughing at me. He called me *normal*. I point at his racket. "But you play a sport *and* do theater."

He laughs again. I made someone laugh. I can't even believe it. I hardly ever talked to the kids when I was in school, because I knew I wouldn't be there long and because, soon enough, they'd see me freak out over a jump rope hitting my leg or a book slamming shut or any of the other thousands of things that happen when I'm around people my age.

Well is talking again. I force myself to pay attention.

"Yeah, I do both. Because I am the well-well-well-rounded Well." He waves the racket around. "And because my dad makes me do both."

The door opens, and Dan ducks his head in.

"There you are! Maxwell, I'd assumed you'd *wait* for me to introduce you, since you begged to stop by."

Well shrugs.

"Maxwell is also in the sixth grade. He lives down the road. I hope, ah, he didn't startle you," Dan says to me. I see him thinking back to Ginger with the blender. I want him to shut up before he says anything that would ruin this. I actually want to say the words "shut up" to an adult.

"No. We're just talking," I say.

"Oh. Good." He looks uncomfortable now, like he doesn't know what role to play here: parent, teacher, or pal. "Maxwell, get your stuff." I guess he's chosen teacher. "I told your dad I'd have you home ten minutes ago."

Well shrugs again.

"He won't notice."

"Go get your stuff anyway. I'll meet you down at the car in *two minutes*."

"All right, Coach. All right."

Well stands as Dan leaves. I stand too, because it feels weird to wave good-bye from the bed. Then, instead of leaving, he picks up Mom's guitar where I left it by the door. No one has touched that guitar but me and Mom. I want to grab it back. What if he messes it up?

"I thought you went by Well," I say, hoping to distract him so he'll put it down.

"It's kind of a new thing."

He's talking, but all I can do is watch his hands on the strings. "I've been at Chickering since kindergarten, so everybody knows me as Maxwell." He pauses, strums an E chord and, to my total amazement, tunes it better than I did. "But let's just say I'm trying to reinvent myself."

"Maxwell!" Dan yells from the foot of the stairs.

"It's a process," he says, and sets the guitar down gently next to the reading chair under the window. Then he holds up a hand for a high five. I look at him, calm as can be, and say, "Catch you later, Well."

"Ohhh, cool as a cucumber," he says as he grabs his racket and moonwalks out. I look over at the guitar.

If a kid like Maxwell can reinvent himself, so can I.

8
We're Going to Be Friends

The outfit is laid out on the reading chair like a murder victim. It is Monday morning at six thirty. School starts at seven forty-five. I cannot possibly put this on. I hold up the blue-and-gray plaid skirt. The white button-down. The navy *sweater vest*. I should have seen this coming. It's fancy private school. Of *course* they have uniforms.

Ginger and I got into our first argument over it yesterday after they got back from church. I didn't go. Being frisked by an airport security guard was nothing compared to the thought of singing hymns and going to Sunday school with a bunch of WWJD kids. Ginger and Dan were fine with that. But when they got home and Ginger pulled out the uniform, still wrapped in cellophane, and I said I wouldn't wear it, *that* was the big deal.

"Lou, you have to wear the uniform."

"I won't. I can't." It was too much. The fabric was stiff, like it had been starched to death, and it made me itch just to touch it.

"Sorry, kiddo. Ginger's right," Dan said as he loosened his tie. It was navy blue with what looked like little yellow bees on it. I leaned closer. Nope, they were tiny Pac-Mans, like from the old video game.

"If you can wear Pac-Man to church, how come I can't wear my sweatshirt to school?"

He rolled up his tie and sighed. "If you want to go to Chickering, you have to be in dress code. Them's the rules. I can't wear Pac-Man to school either, if that makes you feel better."

It didn't.

"Then I'll go to public school."

They both shook their heads.

Ginger said in her lawyer voice, "We've already reg-istered you and informed both Melissa and Maria. If you really are miserable and still want to switch after you give it a few weeks, then we'll go through the nec-essary steps to get you transferred." She wore pearls to church, I noticed.

I was about to say, *Mom wouldn't make me wear a uniform*, and then I realized that's exactly what she does when I put on the dress and boots and suede jacket for performances. It's just that I'm used to that kind of uniform.

Still, I was about to keep arguing. Or take the out-fit and hide it in their big house so no one could ever find it again. But then I thought of Well saying *that's because you're normal*, and I realized I *did* kind of want to go to Chickering. Take theater. Be normal. I looked down at my own outfit. It was *not* normal to wear the same grubby sweatshirt for five days in a row and to be so freaked out about new clothes.

And so, here I am, Monday morning, standing in the middle of the room in a towel, trying to make myself walk over and put on the skirt.

"Lou! Breakfast!"

I place my hand on the shirt. I let it sit there until it doesn't want to jerk away. And then I do the same with the skirt. There's a zipper and hook on the side that I know will freak me out if they brush up against my bare leg. I decide to put the shirt on first and hope it's long enough tucked in to keep the metal off my hip. I dress very slowly, like I'm pulling it on over a bad sunburn. Twenty minutes later I walk stiffly down the stairs and perch on a barstool behind the kitchen counter. It's bearable, just, if I don't think about it too much. But add that to everything *else* I don't want to think about, like starting at a brand-new school partway through the year after not being in a school *at all* in more than a year, and wondering where Mom is waking up today, and there's literally no safe thought in my head.

Ginger turns with cup of coffee in hand when she hears me. "Oh, let me see! Stand up!"

I do, very slowly so the skirt doesn't swish against my skin.

"You look lovely, Lou. Blue really suits you." She's

dressed for work in a black pencil skirt, high heels, and a green sweater. Her hair is twisted up in a knot. She looks like the business version of an American Girl doll. I look like a homeless person in a school uniform, which is exactly what I am. She hands me a banana and a bowl and points to the row of cereal boxes in the pantry.

"Sorry. I'm not really much of a cook. Saturday was an exception." I remember the tomato chunks and say a little prayer of thanks. I walk over to the pantry. Wow. There have to be eight different cereals in here. I pick out a box of Frosted Flakes—name brand!—and then let my eyes wander up the shelves. Organic lentil soup and peanut butter. Some kind of jam with a French label. Whole-wheat pasta and jars of olives and bottles of steak marinades. It's so much food in one place, it takes my breath away. I pick up a package of pink-iced animal crackers.

"Those are my favorite," Ginger says from over my shoulder.

"Mom's too," I say, and crinkle the package in my fingertips. She always lets me have the sprinkles that fall to the bottom of the bag.

Ginger smiles. Her lips are shimmery with pale peach lipstick. "We used to walk to the gas station down the road from our house and buy them with change we found in the couch cushions."

And there it is. Another memory of Mom I never knew. How many times have we eaten these cookies? Why didn't she tell me that story? My stomach clenches, and I put the cookies back. It's not fair. None of this is fair. It's like Mom's a stranger I'm just now being properly introduced to. I sit down with my bowl and pick at the fabric of my skirt under the table. Ginger leans against the counter and sips her coffee. I lean toward the smell.

"Want some?" she asks.

Is this a test? I'm supposed to say no, right? Except I say "yes, please," because I haven't had coffee in *days* and my head hurts and it's not just left over from the concussion. She pours me half a cup and passes me a little carton of fancy creamer—organic cinnamon mocha something or other.

"I probably shouldn't let you, but coffee is one thing I *do* know how to make," she says. We clink our cups together, and I forget about my skirt for a minute.

Dan walks in as I'm rinsing my dishes in the sink, even though Ginger told me to leave them. Who just leaves dirty dishes sitting in the sink? He's wearing khakis with a sharp crease all the way to his loafers. His tie is the same blue-and-gray plaid as my uniform. He lifts a leather satchel over one shoulder. He is the perfect picture of an English teacher.

"Ready to go?" he says.

I grip the edge of the counter, dizzy with fear, even though this part has already been explained to me in detail. Because Chickering is a private school, they don't have buses. Dan will take me to and from school in between tennis practice. Today I will meet with the guidance counselor during first period to go over my schedule and discuss my "school plan" based on the files they sent over from my one year in Biloxi and the few times before that when I actually went to school long enough to have a file. But my insides still turn to Jell-O when he opens the door.

"Wait!" Ginger stops us as we're walking out. "Take this." It's an iPhone.

I look at it in my hand. It is pink with a gold case covered in flowers. "You want me to take your picture?"

"What?" Ginger looks confused. "No! Lou, it's for you. I've programmed in both our cell numbers, and our address is in there too. You just call us if you need us, okay?"

I don't know what to say. It's a brand-new iPhone. I've never had a phone in my life. And now I have an *iPhone* and an iPod. I stop and pat my jacket pocket to check if it's still there. Is this what the rest of the world is like? New phones and music and clothes any time you want them? I take it from her gently like it's a baby bird. It's too much. It would take a year of singing on street corners for change to come close to paying for this. I'm grateful and sad and amazed and confused. I am too many things at once. My throat closes up.

Ginger mistakes my silence for acceptance and moves to hug me. I flinch. She sees it. Her hands hang there in the air like she's paused, until she turns it into a weird two-handed wave.

"Well, have a good day, Lou."

I wave back. "Thanks. I will." Red embarrassment creeps up my neck. Now she'll think I'm ungrateful.

It's just another reminder that I don't know how to be around people other than Mom. And now I have to meet a whole school full of them.

Dan listens to NPR on the way to school. Of course he does. He asks me if I want to change it, but I shake my head. The low voices are kind of relaxing.

We turn down a long driveway lined with magnolias whose leaves are still bright green even on the last day of September. When the driveway opens up to give a full view of the school, I gasp. There's no way this white mansion is a school. But there it is, surrounded by green lawns, tennis courts, a football stadium, and a baseball field. Where's the flat brick building with heavy locked doors? Isn't that what schools are supposed to look like? We keep driving all the way around the back to faculty parking. Even from behind it's beautiful—white-painted brick with turrets and ivy and heavy, dark wood beams. It looks like something out of *The Sound of Music*. I want to crawl under the spare tire in the back.

I sit while Dan gets out of his Jeep, a green dented

thing I bet he's had since college. There are Dave Matthews bumper stickers on the back. He grabs his satchel and his coffee. I am still sitting when he walks over to my window. I can't look at him. I dig my nails into my palms, which are slippery with sweat. Suddenly the zipper on my skirt is way too sharp and tight on my waist. I breathe in short little puffs of air and hum a line from Taylor Swift's "Shake It Off" over and over again.

After a minute or two, Dan motions for me to roll down the window. I crack it open one inch.

"It's okay if you're nervous."

"I'm not nervous."

"Okay. It's okay if you're embarrassed you came to school with a teacher."

"I'm not embarrassed."

He takes a quick sip of coffee and leans against the car. He doesn't know what to do with me. I watch kids walking in. Except for maybe the purses and hair clips, the girls are dressed exactly like me. I look at my skirt. You would never know I lived in a truck a week ago.

"Want to call Ginger?" he asks finally.

I shake my head. I have to pretend like I'm fine, for Mom. I have to be able to handle this, so that when they decide whether to let us live together again, they'll see we are strong, capable people.

I pop the door open, and Dan steps aside as I get out. We both look up at the school, towering in the morning sun.

"It's now or never, kiddo," he says.

Since never's not an option, I grab my backpack, check and double-check my phone and iPod, and follow Dan under the golden crest and into the shining halls of Chickering Academy.

If the outside looks like *The Sound of Music*, the inside looks like Hogwarts. It's all dark wood floors polished so they glow, and the levels open up in a big circle to show the floors above, all the way up to a massive chandelier with little candle-looking lights that have to be fake, because that'd be a fire hazard, right? Above *that* is a skylight that shows the sky still tinged with pink.

"Palatial" is the word that comes to mind from one of the hotel brochures in Tahoe. It's sweeping and epic like a palace, but it's not a palace. It's a middle school, and the high school is an even bigger and fancier version across campus. How am I going to have *anything* in common with these people? What if I scuff up this nice floor with my new shoes? Will I have to switch classes? How will I know where to go? Will there be assigned seats? What if there *literally* isn't a desk for me? I chew at the corner of my thumb and follow Dan into the front office. He points to a big blue sofa, and I sink into it. I want it to swallow me whole. My head throbs and my ears are ringing. I put a fist to my stomach to ease the ache. This was a mistake.

Dan leans against the front desk and starts talking to the secretaries. I've noticed this about him. Along with the knee bobbing, Dan's also a leaner. He leans on everything, like he's too tall to keep himself upright without support. Another few minutes pass where I switch from staring at Dan to staring at my shoes to staring at the clock, anything to keep from having to watch the students walking through the front doors. None of them look at me. I might as well be invisible. I *want* to be invisible. Eventually, after the herd of students passes through, two women walk in, and Dan stands to his full towering height and turns to me and grins. I sink a little farther into the sofa.

"Lou, this is Betty Myers, our principal, and Andrea Scott, our guidance counselor and learning services coordinator."

"Hello, Louise, it is a pleasure," Principal Myers says, and smiles. She is a tall woman, almost as tall as Dan, with short gray hair, and she's dressed in a red pantsuit and bright red lipstick. She looks like a model for Dillard's.

I stand up but look at the floor. "Hello," I say, as if to my shoes.

"Lou, why don't we all move into my office," Ms. Scott says. "They're about to do morning announcements out here."

I follow them around the front desk and down a hallway that is blissfully quiet, just the sounds of a distant copier and a phone ringing from behind a closed door. We walk all the way to the end, into an office that overlooks the football field and the trees behind. There's mist rising from the hills like steam.

It's beautiful. If I could take all my classes in here, alone, it'd be perfect. But of course that's not possible.

I sit in a large cream chair that looks like it should be in the lobby of a hotel somewhere. Instead of going behind her desk, Ms. Scott pulls up a chair so our knees are almost touching. I swivel to the side.

Principal Myers towers above us. "Louise, I have heard so much about you from Dan, and we are excited to have you here at Chickering. I know Ms. Scott will do whatever she can to make sure you feel at home and have the resources you need." This sounds like a speech she's given before. "And now, without further ado, we'll leave you two to get acquainted," she says, and then snaps her fingers at Dan. "And you, sir, have a homeroom class awaiting your presence." She sounds a little frightening, but Dan just smiles at her like he's used to it.

"I'm on it, I'm on it," he says, and adjusts his satchel on his shoulder, preparing to go. But as they're both walking out, he turns and says, "You're going to be just fine, Lou. I promise. I'll come find you at lunch." So it's not total abandonment. But it sure feels like it once I'm alone with Ms. Scott.

I spend thirty seconds tracing the lines on my skirt with a fingernail because I don't know what to do next.

Then Ms. Scott says, "You can call me Andrea," and I make myself look up. She's sifting through papers, my file, I guess, so I let myself study her. If there is a total opposite to Principal Myers, it's Andrea. For one thing, she's short, shorter than me, maybe. With her long braid and no makeup, she looks kind of like a hippie gnome.

"Lou," she says, tapping a pen on one of the sheets she's laid out on the big ottoman next to us. "It looks like you did fairly well in your last school. Croft Elementary in . . . Biloxi, right?"

I nod.

I *am* good at school, when I get the chance to go.

"Grammar, reading, math, science"—she moves her pen down the page—"all within average to above-average range. However—" And here she stops and looks up at me over a pair of square, purple glasses. "The counselor there noted several behavioral incidents, during music and recess, where you had to be removed from the rest of the class?"

I remember those "incidents." There was the day in music when the teacher passed out cymbals and everybody slammed them together all at once, over and over, until it felt like my eardrums would explode and I ran screaming into the corner. And recess. Jump-rope games I wouldn't join because I couldn't handle the feel of the rope slapping my legs if I missed. And the swings. The creak of those rusted swings was so loud I hid under the slide until everyone had gone inside. They let me sit with the teacher most days after that.

So much for faking normal. All the junk has followed me here.

"Lou, it's okay. I promise. I've seen this before," Andrea claims.

It was the same thing Maria said, but I saw how spooked she was on the plane. I saw how totally *out of her element* she was with someone like me, because there *is* no one else like me. I pick back up where I left off, following the pattern on my skirt.

"Lou, listen. I used to be an occupational therapist in my former life. Do you know what that is?"

I shake my head.

"It's like a physical therapist, except an occupational therapist is someone who helps kids do the things in their everyday lives they find extra hard. I helped them with fine motor skills like eating and coloring and writing with a pencil."

"I know how to eat. And color." It sounds snotty, but she just said I was smart, so why does she think I need to learn how to hold a pencil?

"I also helped a lot of kids who were extra sensitive to certain things—textures of food and fabric, physical contact with other people, unexpected noise."

Oh.

She reaches over and hands me a sheet of paper. "I know we've just met, but would you do something for me, Lou?" She pushes her glasses up her nose. "We have thirty-five minutes until the bell rings for the next class. Will you try answering these questions as honestly as you can? There's no right or wrong here. I just want you to do your best."

When she stands, she's not much taller than me sitting. It's hard to be intimidated by that, so I murmur "okay," and she moves to the door. Her long braid swings behind her like a kid. "I'll give you some privacy."

I look down at the paper in my hand and read *Adolescent Sensory Questionnaire.*

Great.

The memory of Mrs. Guidry's whispered words comes back. Already someone's trying to label me. If Mom were here, she'd pitch a fit. But that never got us anywhere either. Just requests from the school for testing, followed by a quick exit from town. With a start, I realize that maybe Mom's way wasn't the best.

I dig a pencil out of my bag and begin. I'm supposed to check the ones that apply:

___ *bothered by "light touch," someone lightly touching your hand, face, leg, or back*

___ *distressed by others touching you*

I check both, but they seem like the same thing, which is a little unfair. Also, who isn't a little creeped out by "light touch"? I move down the list.

___ *have to fidget and "fiddle" with things all the time:*

change in your pocket, your keys, a pen/pencil, paper
clip, rubber band, anything within reach

I almost don't check this one, but then I think of the iPod, the phone, the fringe on my suede jacket, the guitar case, and I have to scratch an *X* next to this one too.

__ *often touching and twisting your own hair*

Well yeah. Of course. But that can't be weird. Every girl does that, right?

__ *feel uncomfortable wearing new or "stiff" clothes that*
have not been washed or soaked in fabric softener

I look down at my skirt and sigh.

__ *drink excessive amounts of coffee or caffeinated beverages*

I think of the coffee this morning and all the coffee that has come before it. But I disagree on the "excessive" part. I'm not marking that one.

__ *notice and bothered by noises other people do not seem bothered by: clocks, refrigerators, fans, people talking, outdoor construction, etc.*

__ *sensitive to loud sounds or commotion*

I think of the blender, horns honking, the airplane engine, the cymbals in music class, the creaky swings.

__ *cannot attend certain public events or places due to excessive noise*

__ *avoid crowds and plan errands at times when there will be fewer people*

__ *hide or disappear when guests come over*

This is every single public performance. Every time I had to get up in front of people and sing. Every karaoke stage. Every farmer's market. Every street corner. I drop the pencil and start to cry.

I want my mom.

I'm trying to find a tissue on Andrea's desk so I can blow my nose. It's an avalanche of papers and Post-its, and there's even a half-knitted scarf. Then I spot them next to a framed picture of a dog in reindeer antlers. I bump into her keyboard when I reach for one. The computer springs to life with a burst of sunflower background. The screen is cluttered with icons. But it's not asking for a password. I take a breath. And then another. Because I have an idea.

It takes one Google search to find Bagels and Joe in Tahoe City. I can't believe I didn't think of this the minute Ginger handed me the phone this morning. I dig it out of my pocket and dial with one hand while blowing my nose with the other.

It rings.

And rings.

I'm about to hang up when there's a click and a man's voice.

"Bagels and Joe. Joe here."

I hear the clink of cups and hiss of the steamer from the espresso machine in the background. I close my eyes and see it. The warped wood floors and coffee beans shelved as neatly as library books.

"Hi, Joe," I say after a minute.

He lets out a little whoosh of air. It's a staticky wind down the line. "Lou. Oh man. You okay?"

The sound of him makes me happy and sad at the same time. "Yeah. I'm all right."

"Where are you? The lady from the child services didn't say."

"Maria? She came by?"

"Yeah, and the police."

I swallow hard.

"What'd they want?"

"They just wanted to know what I thought about your mom. Asked me if they thought she was looking out for you. Asked me how you seemed."

"What'd you say?"

He pauses so long I check the phone to see if we've been disconnected.

"I said I thought she was probably doing the best she could. And that you seemed okay. Maybe a little lonely."

I close my eyes. Was it that obvious?

"How's my mom? Have you seen her?"

"Lou, I'm not supposed to talk to you about this."

"Please, Joe. They won't even tell me where she is."

He sighs. I wait. Someone yells out an order for a cappuccino in the background. Heavy on the foam.

"She's doing okay. She's bunking down with Amelie."

"Who?"

"Amelie, the manager from Christy's."

The one who chased us off when I had that last meltdown? The one Mom yelled at as we were walking away from the crowd, me with gravel still in my knees? Now they're buddies?

"But—"

"Lou, she's trying real hard to get on her feet. The truck's in the shop, but it'll be a while."

If she's got a place to stay and is "getting on her feet," why hasn't she called? I can't talk anymore. The ache in my stomach is back.

"Okay, thanks, Joe."

I start to hang up but hear him say right before I can press end, "Hang in there, Lou. And, uh, check in every now and then, okay?"

"Okay."

I put the phone in my pocket and toss the tissue in the trash. By the time Andrea comes back, I'm in my chair with the form facedown in my lap. She takes it without looking at it and walks me to second period with an easy smile. I pretend to be normal. I stick to the plan. But inside I feel something crumbling. The picture of who I thought Mom was is falling apart.

Well is waiting outside math class. I stop short. It's enough to distract me from what Joe said. Is Well waiting for me? He was so nice the other day, but I figured that was just him and I was nothing special. He'd probably make friends with a tree. But now he's holding out his arm like he's asking me to dance. Today his nails are black.

"Um . . . ," I manage when he doesn't move.

"I'm trying to be *gallant*," he whispers. I smile a tiny bit even though it hurts a little. I'm still not taking his arm, though. My body wouldn't let me even if I tried. Luckily, he turns the whole thing into a bow so low that his tie drags on the floor.

"After you, miss," he says as I pass by.

It turns out Well's in both math and geography with me, and I am better than him at both. Mom is terrible with money. She handed our tiny budget over to me a long time ago. And as the designated "navigator," I've spent a lot of time with a map on my lap. The best part is that I don't have to do the standard "stand in front of the class and tell us about yourself" routine that every other school has made me do. These teachers are all business. Roll call and get to work. Maybe that's what middle school is like, or maybe they just know that every twelve-year-old's worst nightmare is to stand alone in front of everybody else. With the exception of Well. I bet Well would introduce himself every day if he got the chance.

Even though it isn't as terrible as I thought it would be, and Well stays next to me through second and third period, and the bells between classes sound like wind chimes and so don't startle me at all . . . even then, by lunch, I am shaky and tired. I forgot what it was like to be around so many people my age. As promised, Dan is waiting for me in front of the cafeteria when I come down the stairs with Well. It's on the bottom floor and opens onto a grassy area with picnic tables.

"Maxwell, thank you for showing Lou around."

"Oh, it's a pleasure, Coach. Lou is the first new kid in our grade in about three years. Tour guide is a new gig for me." He puts on a game-show voice and turns to me. "And to your right, you'll see our lovely dining hall. You better not call it the lunchroom, because lunchrooms don't have homemade chai granola and a smoothie bar!"

"Seriously?" I ask, because surely not.

"Seriously," he says, and Dan nods. My last school had pizza and Fritos and ice cream cups that had melted and refrozen so often by the time you opened one, there was just nothing there.

"We had fish sticks back in my day," Dan says. "You'd think San Diego could do better than that with seafood." That Dan is from California is news to me. I try to picture him surfing on a Saturday morning or hitting up the skate park in the afternoon. Or bumming a ride out to Tahoe on the weekend to snowboard. I just can't see it. He seems so much more at home in his ties with the crossword puzzle tucked under his arm.

While I'm squinting at him, trying to picture him with sunglasses and a tan, he hands me a small plastic card that looks like a credit card. It has my name printed on it and the same gold crest as the school.

"This card links to your student account. You can use it to get lunch, anything out of the vending machines, and clothes or school supplies from the Bird's Nest."

I stare at it. My very own kid-size credit card. I wonder how much Dan put on it and how I will ever pay him back.

"What's the Bird's Nest?" I ask instead.

"Don't worry about it," Well says, not looking up from my new phone, where he is adding himself as a contact. "It's the school pep store. I am *not* letting you buy a single thing with a crest or a bird on it. Ridiculous."

"Why a bird?"

"We're the Chickering Sparrows. That's our mascot," Dan explains, pointing to the giant gray bird painted above the doors leading outside to the picnic tables.

"Worst mascot ever," Well says, and swipes the card from me. "Come on, Lou. I'll take it from here, Coach."

"You kids have fun. And keep an eye on the clock. Fourth period starts in twenty-eight minutes."

"Oodles of time. Let's go."

I follow Well between the tables and try not to make eye contact with anyone. But most people are texting or doing homework, so nobody looks up.

"Lunch is the only time we can have our phones out during school," Well says when he sees me staring. Am I the only kid here who didn't own a phone until today?

We wind our way past the smoothie and salad bars, the baked potato and soup stations, and a prepared-food line. It's like a tiny supermarket. We stop at the end by the cash register, and Well grabs two Snickers ice cream bars from a deep freezer and a bag of Doritos off the rack. He piles them all up in front of the lunch lady and hands her his card.

"My treat," he says.

"Oh no, I can't." Just one of those ice cream bars is four dollars at the gas station. How much more can I possibly owe people?

"Oh please," Well says, waving me off as I try to hand the cafeteria lady my card. Which, if I think about it, isn't any different than Well paying. I'm loaded down with everybody else's money. At least when I sang, I *earned* the quarters and dimes and dollars. "That's money to your name, Lou," Mom would say.

Well ignores my offer to buy tomorrow's lunch and leads us back toward the tables. I hold my breath to see which is "his table," but he keeps walking until we reach the doors that open onto the lawn.

"Where are we going?" I ask when he doesn't stop at the picnic tables.

He arches an eyebrow at me. "Where the cool kids eat, of course."

As we cut across the baseball field, I watch my saddle shoes turn orange from the dugout dirt and try to breathe normally at the thought of meeting

Well's friends. He's heading toward the football stadium. Even from a hundred yards away I can see three kids sitting in the bleachers, and I freeze, right in the middle of the outfield.

I've *just* started getting comfortable around Well. Other people, though . . . What if they ask me about my mom? Or what my old school was like? What if they make a joke about my skinny bird legs? Or what if they do something crazy like run up and down the bleachers? The sound of that *bang, bang, bang* of feet on metal is a bad one for me. More than a shiver. More like a scream.

"Why'd you stop?" Well asks, a few feet ahead now.

"I, uh, I think I'm going to go back in. I don't want to be late for fourth period."

"No. Uh-uh. Fourth period is theater, and I make it a habit to be fashionably late. Besides, see those jokers? They're in theater too. We can all be late, *or on time*," he adds when he sees me start to turn away, "together."

"No, really. I'm going back."

"Lou, stop or I swear to God I will eat your ice cream bar."

I stop.

"Now sit down."

I look at the wet grass covered in leaves. "What? Here?"

"Yes, here."

Well takes off his navy school jacket and spreads it on the ground. He sits, then pats a spot next to him. When I keep standing, he unwraps both Snickers ice cream bars and holds one up under my nose, like a bouquet of roses. I sit.

"Now listen." He hands me the Doritos to open. "I was saving this for later, because it felt like a perfect end-of-the-first-day thing to do, but you have forced my hand, Lou." He looks at me from under a fringe of black hair. "So, if it falls flat, that is on *you*. Do you get me?"

"I do," I say. Except I don't, because I have no idea what he's talking about. And I hate surprises for obvious reasons.

He pulls a phone from his pocket. I watch him scrolling through his music and can't stop myself from leaning in to see what's on his list.

"This, Louie Lou, is the Spotify app, which I noticed you do not yet have on your phone, and we will fix that posthaste, but for right now I am going to play you a song and you are going to love it, okay? Here," he says, plugging in his earbuds and handing me one. "Don't worry, they're clean."

I don't take it at first. What if it's death metal or screaming punk? What if I literally curl into a ball and cry at the first note?

He sighs. "Just *trust* me, okay?"

I don't trust him. Not yet. But I do put the earbud in as he puts in the other, because right now Well is my only maybe-friend and I can't lose that. I watch him click play and cross my fingers I don't freak out.

It starts off easy enough. A simple guitar solo. And then I hear a tenor voice. High and sweet as summer. It's a guy singing about going back to school in the fall. He meets a friend. They climb a fence and walk to the park. "Walk with me, Suzy Lee," he sings, and I look over at Well. He's smiling and nodding along and biting into his ice cream bar. A piece of chocolate falls onto his shirt collar. I close my eyes to listen better.

Simple strumming. Simple melody. It's beautiful.

I let it play all the way until the end before I open my eyes. And when I do, I feel calm and happy—that mood that only music can make. How did Well know? I turn to ask him, but he's opening and closing his mouth without saying anything.

"What?" I yank the earbud out, panicking, because even though I haven't known him long, I know a speechless Well is *not* normal.

"You, Lou, have been hiding something."

He points a black fingernail at me.

"What? No!" I shake my head.

"Yes. Oh *yes*," he says.

Whatever he's about to say can't be good. I have no good secrets. Just embarrassing or terrifying ones. I get up, let the earbud fall onto his jacket, and start to go.

"Wait!" he shouts, and runs after me.

I speed up. And so does he until he's speed-walking next to me.

He holds up his phone and blurts, "You, Louise, can *sing*."

I stop, confused.

"What?"

He shakes his phone at me, like it holds all the answers.

"You were singing out loud," he says.

"Oh, that." I didn't even know I was doing it.

"Yes, *that*. You're like a bluesy lounge singer hiding in Tinker Bell's body," Well says, sounding impressed.

I have no idea how to respond to this, so I settle for finishing my ice cream bar.

"Stop staring at me," I say.

"I can't. You might be the next American Idol."

I turn away, but then I'm facing the bleachers again, and there's nothing left to do but start walking toward them, because it's better than Well staring at me like I just levitated.

"How can we not talk about this?" Well says, catching up.

"There's nothing to talk about."

"*Nothing to talk about?* You are a diva!"

"No, I'm not."

I walk faster, so he has to jog.

"Fine. I'm just . . . *impressed.*"

"It's a good song."

"It *is* a good song, a great song, by the White Stripes, which is now officially epic, thanks to you. My dad hates it, though. He only listens to country."

I laugh. Finally, something we have in common.

"Yeah, my mom, too."

"Oh yeah?"

It's the first time I've mentioned Mom, and I can tell he's waiting for me to say more. But he lets it go when I don't. Instead, right before we get to the bleachers, he says, "The reason I played you that song . . . this was before I realized you were actually Tina Turner . . . is that I'm glad I met you. You're my Suzy Lee, get it?"

I do not. He barely knows me. And it could either be super creepy or super sweet. But I think of all those lonely days, just me and Mom, and all the random schools where I never even got close to being friends with anybody, and I think, *Yeah, I kind of* do *get it.* Because it'd be nice to be someone's person and you wouldn't have to do anything other than just be you. I shake my head. Well is probably the kind of guy who has tons of friends, like the ones on the bleachers currently waving blue and silver pom-poms. Actual pom-poms. This is just Well being Well.

"Dude, check these out! Found them under the bleachers!" a kid who looks big enough to be an eighth grader yells from where he's lying on his back on the bottom row, shaking pom-poms like maracas. He gives me an upside-down grin.

Well begins the introductions: "Lou, this is Tucker. Tucker is a gentle giant and would rather snuggle up with a casserole than do any kind of physical exercise. But he's not bad in the props department, which is why we let him hang with us."

"I'll have you know I'm in training," upside-down Tucker says, and pretends to bench-press his pom-poms.

"Yeah? For what? Cheerleading tryouts?" says Well, and grabs one of them. What's the singular for pom-poms? Pom?

"No." He sits up and tugs the ends of his curly blond hair behind his ears. It's just long enough. "Hot-dog-eating contest at the end of October."

"Really?" I say despite my shyness. I watched one of those at a county fair we were working two years ago. The winner ate sixty-three hot dogs in ten minutes.

"He does not lie," says the girl sitting one row up from Tucker. I take a step back, closer to Well. Girls make me more nervous than guys. They are sneakier at teasing.

"This lovely green-haired goddess is Geneva," announces Well. "She's just finished a stint as a fairy in *A Midsummer Night's Dream* at the performing arts center downtown. It's the only reason the school let her dye her lovely locks."

Geneva stands and gives a salute. There's a half-finished bird drawn on her wrist. "Hiya, Lou. Maxwell here has talked a lot about you in the last forty-eight hours. A lot. So I'm glad you're here, and he can finally shut up."

I look at Well and he shrugs.

"When are you going to start calling me Well?" he asks Geneva.

"When I've known you as many years as Well as I have as Maxwell. So"—she pretends to look at her watch—"six years and counting."

"Whatever." Well turns to the only person who has yet to look at me. "That geek over there with the laptop who is completely ignoring us is Jacob. Jacob is a budding sound engineer who also likes to play Dungeons and Dragons in his spare time with his virtual friends."

Jacob's technically in uniform, but just barely. I see a red T-shirt peeking out from under his collar, and his Sperrys have neon-green laces. "Don't knock it," he says without looking up. "I still catch you there on a Saturday night."

Well totally ignores this and turns back to me.

"And this, Lou, is pretty much the sixth-grade division of the theater department. We hold our own."

I turn to him. "What do *you* do in theater?"

"Me?" Well puts a hand to his chest. "I act, of course. *I* am a thespian."

Tucker throws his other pom at him. And Geneva, after checking her watch for real this time, adds, "You're about to be a tardy thespian. We all are if we don't make a run for it."

Somehow, and one of these days I'm going to figure out how, I managed to get through a traumatic self-help test, three classes, and lunch without actually thinking about the fact that I had signed up and would eventually have to go to an *acting* class.

But when I walk into the dance studio where theater is held, I realize I am in serious trouble, and all the panic that had stayed barely in check since I walked in this morning comes flooding out. I can't *act*. I spend every minute of every set Mom and I do pretending I'm invisible. I have to get out of here.

Well, Geneva, Tucker, and Jacob are ahead of me. We are the only sixth graders in the class, and it's the only class in the middle school that combines grades. The seventh and eighth graders are sitting in groups by the huge wall-to-wall mirror texting and putting on makeup. I cannot do this. I start to breathe a little too fast. I take a step backward. I've got one foot in the door and one foot out. Nobody sees. If I make it to the hallway, I will run. I will run straight to Andrea's office and plead temporary insanity and sign up for something safe like knitting.

Just one. More. Step.

I back into someone, and it's enough to make me scream.

"You've got a set of lungs on you, sweetheart!"

I turn around to see a woman who looks like one of the fortune-tellers outside the casinos in Biloxi. Her hair is fluffed out all over like a dandelion, and her hoop earrings are as big as the bangles on her arms. She studies me and hmmms. "Look at those eyes. You could be a fawn in a forest, my dear. Now why don't you shimmy on in so we can get started?"

I want to get *out*, not farther in. My heart's still jumping. But it's either take a seat next to Well or physically push past her, and that would mean touching. I shuffle off to the side, and Well grins. I swallow and taste Dorito all over again.

"For those of you who are new"—she pauses to wink at me—"I am Mrs. Nicole Russo. Mrs. Nicky, for short. And today is *movement* day. By the end of the week, we'll wrap up casting for *Into the Woods*, our winter musical. And remember"—she snaps her fingers and I wince, just a little, not enough so you'd notice—"if you make it past round one, round two auditions are Thursday at four in the gym. *Do not be late.* It's unprofessional. Now—" She snaps again, but

I stay still. I was ready that time. I make a mental note: Mrs. Nicky is a snapper. "Take off your shoes and stretch those toes and roll those shoulders and loosen your mind. No thoughts today. Only movement and music and . . . *physicality*."

"Aleeeeeexa!" she singsongs, calling roll, I guess. But nobody answers. She says it again louder. "Alexa, play a rrrrrrumba!" She rolls her *r*s and her hips at the same time. I look toward the piano, but there's nobody there. Then a little hockey puck on the piano bench lights up and says in a creepy voice, "Playing Rumba Playlist from Amazon top picks."

"What was *that*?" I whisper to Well as Spanish dance music thrums across the open space.

Well is already balling his socks, light purple with yellow stars, into his shoes and not looking at me. "*This*, Suzy Lee, is the rumba. Think Ricky Martin meets Carlos Santana."

"No, I mean *that*." I point at the hockey puck.

Well's mouth falls open and I know I've just said something dumb, but I have no idea what, and then he bursts into laughter so hard he actually has to bend over. Is he laughing at me? My cheeks flush red, and my pulse picks up all over again.

He stands up and wipes his eyes. "Are you telling me you don't know Alexa? The first world's answer to to-do lists and Google searches and mood music and any kind of simple math? Oh, Lou. What basement have you been hiding in?"

I cringe. What would he say if he knew it was actually a truck?

Jacob leans forward on the other side of Well, where he was typing away on his laptop again, and says, "Pay no attention to him. Alexa is for people who can't find their way out their own front door without directions."

"So, perfect for Max, then," Geneva says, and glides her way onto the dance floor with her arms lifted like a belly dancer. Tucker slams Jacob's laptop shut with his foot and then runs off when Jacob chases him.

"Sorry, I was just teasing. It's a thing I do. But I'm working on it. I'm in a twelve-step program." Well holds his hand out to me and nods toward the dance floor. "Let me make it up to you?"

My throat closes up. I cannot even pretend to do this. I shake my head. Well mistakes it for the first dance move and starts to shake his head too. No. He's not getting it. I shake my head harder. And he shakes his *back*. He thinks I'm *dancing* with him. Then Jacob, who has chased Tucker in a full circle around the room, knocks into Well, who smacks into me, and I *cannot take it another second.*

I push Well hard and run out. Alexa and the rumba echo down the hall, and I can't get far enough away. I stumble and trip on one of my shoelaces. My knee drags across the carpet in a slow burn that rubs off the skin. The pain clears my head enough for me to look up and search for an exit. I am in the middle of the hallway. I need to get somewhere private. And quick.

By the time Mrs. Nicky finds me in the bathroom, I am holding a wet paper towel over my knee and breathing normally.

"So, not a fan of the rumba, then?" She leans

against the wall and crosses her arms. She's blocking the only exit, and I have to fight the instinct to push her like I did Well.

"No, ma'am. It's not that. I've just got a headache." I point to the concussion bump, still yellow and purple on my temple.

"Ahhh." She leans forward. "A bit ghoulish." She studies my head and then my skinned knee. "I'd like to see the other guy." She comes closer, earrings and silver bracelets jangling. I back up until I feel the paper towel dispenser poke into my spine. She cocks her head at me.

"Listen, Lou, I'm going to be straight with you. Theater's not for the faint of heart."

She's giving me an out. She can see I'm not like everybody else. I'm weird in a way that isn't theater-kid cool. I'm not eccentric. She's right. I'm "faint of heart."

I picture everyone dancing and laughing while I stand in this bathroom with a stupid paper towel on my leg. It's not fair. I don't *want* to be this way. Ten minutes ago I would have taken Mrs. Nicky's chance to drop the class in a heartbeat. But now, I'm . . . What am I? I'm *angry*.

"I'll be out in a minute."

For a split second she looks pleased, like this is what she'd been after all along. But then it's gone, so I can't be sure. "All right, then. Let's do this." She throws open the door but turns back to say, "I'll give you a hint. Dance number two is a bluesy number. Think of all your heart's aches, those bumps and bruises of the soul, and let them *propel* you across the dance floor." Then she's gone.

So, after apologizing to Well for "needing some air," which he doesn't even question because he's too busy dancing, I slide my feet from side to side in the corner of the dance studio. For exactly two minutes and thirteen seconds, I shuffle to the tune of a very sad trumpet. I am, at least for now, a theater kid.

9
Everything's Okay

I'm sitting on top of Ginger and Dan's dryer listening to Patsy Cline sing about how she's crazy for feeling so lonely, and I'm thinking about Mom, again. I've called Joe's a hundred times to check up on her since Monday, but I always hang up. I shouldn't have to be the one who checks in. That's *her* job.

She used to always make me sing Patsy Cline at the state fairs, the same ones that have the hot-dog-eating contests. State fairs are the poor person's beauty pageant. You can sign up to sing at the last minute, and everyone'll loan you their hairspray and handkerchiefs.

It's heavy on the country music and also, weirdly, on the Disney solos. There were Patsy Clines and Dolly Partons, but also a lot of Queen Elsas and Ariels. Patsy takes me back to hot funnel cakes and face-painting stands and pony rides. There were also BB-gun shots from the target booth and the clanging metal of the Tilt-A-Whirl and the *ding! ding! ding!* when someone hit the top of the Test Your Strength game, but I don't like to think of those.

The dryer switches cycles under my legs, and I miss the nights with Mom at the Laundromat. The rumbling and whirring noises were soothing, and it was always warm in the winter. Also, nobody talks to anybody. You come to clean your clothes, not socialize.

Mom would read or do a puzzle from her jumbo sudoku book, and I'd listen to music on our portable CD player and make towers out of the quarters we kept in a ziplock baggie labeled *Clean Me Fund*. When I was *really* little, I'd burrow under the still-warm clothes Mom dumped back in the laundry basket. I smelled like lavender fabric softener the rest of the day.

Ginger comes in now and hops up next to me. It takes her a few tries to do it. It's eight o'clock on Thursday night, but she just got home. Apparently, estate law is a needy business with needy people who keep you on call just to answer questions like, *Is the plane privately owned or part of the company's assets?* And if it is part of the company's assets, *Does that mean I shouldn't have used it to fly my son to his college visit at Princeton?* Seriously. That call had Ginger out the door at six this morning.

She hands me a half-opened package of the pink animal crackers and takes a handful for herself.

"Did you get dinner?" she asks, letting her high heels slide off and fall to the floor.

"Yeah. Dan picked up Chinese."

"Good."

She closes her eyes and leans back. The vibration of the machine makes her shoulders shake, and she smiles. "You know, your mom and I used to do this too. We'd sit on the dryer and trade Baby-Sitters Club books until your grandma shooed us off."

"Mom never told me that," I say, and feel another

frizzle of anger. The more I learn about Mom, the less I understand her.

"Your grandma wasn't all bad. She made the best blackberry cobbler I have ever eaten." Ginger sighs and bites into an animal cracker. "I think," she says, pausing to chew, "she just didn't know what to do with us. She expected we'd stay close, get jobs like hers working at the Burlington Coat Factory. When I got a scholarship, she said college was 'above my station,' and if I went, I shouldn't come back to rub their noses in it." She shakes her head. "I tried once, you know, to go see them my senior year. Their car was parked out back, and I saw the curtains move when I knocked. But they never answered the door."

"That's terrible."

She rubs the back of her neck, then rolls down the top of the package of animal crackers in tiny, perfect folds.

"That's just them."

That doesn't sound like much of an excuse to me. I think about Mom not even calling and thump the dryer with my heel.

"You know, your grandpa was on disability the whole time we were growing up. He injured his back on a construction job. When they found out your mom was pregnant, they lost it. If I was above my station, well, Jill had sunk too far below. They said they couldn't possibly take on another mouth to feed and she'd have to get a job with your grandma if she wanted the two of you to stay. So Jill left."

Wait. What? Mom always told me she'd been kicked out. If what Ginger just said is true, then this means she had a choice. She *chose* to leave. She chose to keep us separate and not let me meet my grandparents, however awful they might be. Or Ginger. All those places. All those schools I never got to finish. She always chose to leave. I bang my heels against the dryer, this time hard enough to sting. But it's not hard enough to make the hurt go away.

"You don't have to do that, you know?" Ginger says, and I jump. I forgot she was there.

"Do what?"

"Your laundry. Just leave it in the basket, and I can take care of it."

"It's okay. I like to do it."

"All right, then." Ginger smiles and hops down. "I'm off to eat some cold beef and broccoli."

A few minutes later, the dryer buzzes, and I pull out my old jeans and new school shirts. There have been about a hundred times in the week, when my phone lights up with a text from Well or I wake up in my blue room or I swipe my student card in the vending machine to get a Twix, not because I'm starving, but just because I can, that I think about how different my life is now than it was in Tahoe. But even with all the new stuff and friends and family, I still would have chosen to go back to Mom. Now, after what Ginger just told me, I'm not so sure.

Friday morning is rainy and cold. The kind of cold that slinks down your jacket collar and settles into your skin. It's been one week. One week of Chickering Academy and uniforms and algebra equations and English with Dan, where I have to call him Mr. Latimer, and theater with Mrs. Nicky, which, luckily for me, isn't all like Monday's class. There's book work too. We're in the history of vaudeville right now.

But today I have to meet with Andrea again. She wants to talk about the questionnaire. Dan leaves me at her door at seven fifteen. We have half an hour for her to talk at me and me to stare at the floor. I don't want to know what my answers to her questions mean. If I don't know, whatever it is can't be true.

"Lou, come in! Come in!" Andrea chirps. With her hair down, it's almost as long as mine. She's wearing a denim dress and scuffed boots. Mom would approve. "Can I get you something to drink? Tea? Water?" she asks.

She doesn't mention coffee. I wonder what age I have to be for it to be acceptable to be offered coffee? I miss Joe. But at least her office is warm, and there's a candle lit. I sniff. Lavender. It's supposed to be calming, but it's not doing the trick. Whatever the answers to those questions were supposed to be, I marked them wrong. And this is how she's going to break it to me. With tea and lavender.

"Lou, I've had a chance to look at the questionnaire you filled out for me on Monday."

"I failed, right?"

"What? No, honey. This isn't about passing or failing. And your teachers say you've been doing excellent work in class. We're just gathering data. That's all this is."

"But . . ."

"No 'but.' This is an 'and' conversation. *And*, based on the questionnaire, it seems that certain situations trigger some anxiety in you. *And* that's what we're here to talk about." She leans back in her chair, picks up her own cup of tea, and smiles. Like everything's all good.

I remember the whispers of those teachers in fourth grade and feel ten all over again. I've been doing really well so far. I finish my homework and eat lunch with Well and Tucker and Jacob and Geneva. I even spoke during class discussion in Dan's class, though I didn't want to. But none of it matters. "Let me guess. I'm 'on the spectrum,'" I say, using air quotes.

"You mean are you autistic? No, not necessarily." Andrea puts her cup down and pauses to push up her glasses. "Lou, you can't determine that from one test. You would need to meet with a pediatrician and therapist, be observed by your teachers and family, take some other, different kinds of tests in our learning center. All that would need to happen before any official diagnosis."

I slump back in my chair. I am one part relieved and one part super confused. So what does this mean? Something's wrong, but it's not what they thought? Is this worse? Is it worse to have something nobody understands? I tug at the ends of my hair. They're wet from the rain. I find a knot and yank.

"So, is there a name for it? Whatever your questionnaire was asking about?"

Andrea takes a second before she answers. I've noticed this about her. She's never in a rush to fill in silences, unlike Mom, who can't stand the quiet, even for one second.

"Well, there are different forms, and no two cases look the same, but yes, from what I've seen as an occupational therapist and what you've answered on the questionnaire, I'd say you have a sensory processing disorder. SPD. And if you give me your pediatrician's contact information, I'd like to put a call in to him or her to work on getting you an appointment set up with a practicing occupational therapist. Then, if they agree that this is in fact SPD, we can start building a good learning plan."

I yank at the knot in my hair again. Sensory. Processing. Disorder. SPD. SPD. SPD. *SPDSPDSPD-SPDSPD,* I say over and over in my head until it stops making sense. Because it *doesn't* make sense. I've been here a week, and they already want to "fix" me. Mom wouldn't tolerate it.

"I don't want a plan," I say, and twist my skirt in my hands. It's not as itchy now that I doused it in fabric softener and washed it ten times.

"Okay." Andrea sips her tea. "Why not?"

"This is dumb. You just said I'm doing fine in school, excellent even." I pause to channel my inner Mom. "I don't want you to tell my teachers that I have some *disorder,*" I say, and add to myself, *Because teachers are terrible at keeping secrets and I finally have friends for the first time in my life and I'd like to keep it that way.*

"Lou, this is not as uncommon as you think. Five to fifteen percent of kids have some form of a sensory processing disorder." She's trying to make this no big deal, like how people talk about having ADHD. But I've seen the kids who really have ADHD. I've seen what it's like for them when they forget their meds. It's a huge deal.

I shake my head.

Andrea puts her tea down. "But, Lou, what happens at the pep rallies? The cheering, the yelling . . . the blowing horns? What happens in science class when you have to stand shoulder to shoulder with your lab partner and do an experiment? What happens in the dining hall if the checkout line gets jammed, and everyone's jostling to pay?" She pauses. "What happens then?"

I sit back in the chair and close my eyes. Every one of those scenarios is my worst nightmare, and Andrea knows it. She keeps talking.

"No one is doubting that you have done an excellent job coping all these years. But, Lou, not everything has to be so hard. My job is to help you get the most out of your educational experience. We can make accommodations. We can make it easier."

You are a fighter. I hear Mom's words again like she's right here. I think of Well and sharing headphones on the wet grass. Of dancing to the blues with Mrs. Nicky. Of sitting on the dryer eating cookies with Ginger. The minute I let Andrea tell everyone about this, it'll all be over. I'll be the "special-needs kid." The kid with the disorder. My chance at normal will disappear. Fighters keep fighting.

I open my eyes and sit up.

"I don't want a plan."

Melissa, the caseworker, is standing next to her motorcycle, waiting for our end of the week check-in when Dan pulls down the drive this afternoon. I go straight up to my room without looking at her. This day has been a boatload of badness. After my meeting with Andrea, we had a memory exercise in theater. Mrs. Nicky made us close our eyes and sniff different things to see what it made us remember. She said smell is the number one sense linked to memory.

We had to smell damp leaves, a spotty banana, and a leather shoe. Big deal. But then she passed around a box filled with coins. Most people don't realize money has a smell, but it does. The minute I breathed in the flat, metallic scent, I saw myself squatting in front of the guitar case in Lexington, Conway, Biloxi, Tahoe, and a dozen other cities, separating nickels and dimes and quarters. I could feel the baggie that held the quarters for our laundry fund. Someone gave us a two-dollar coin once and I wanted to save it, but Mom said we needed it for gas money. Your hands smell after you handle money too, the same stink as the hangers at Goodwill. I bet nobody in all of Chickering Academy knows that smell. When the bell rang at the end of class, I walked out without looking at anybody.

Ginger calls from the bottom of the stairs. I take a deep breath and peer out over the landing. They all look up at me from the sofa. Ginger must have taken off work early. I know Dan's skipping his own tennis practice. This is a big meeting. I want to climb out my window and hide on the roof.

"Long time no see," Melissa says when I come in after walking as slowly as possible down the stairs. I am aiming at slothlike speed. She's in all black again. I wonder if she owns anything else.

I sit down next to Ginger. This is just another test.

"I spoke with your school today. Seems like things are off to a good start?"

She wants me to elaborate. I don't.

"Yes, Lou's doing great in my class," Dan says, sounding way too chipper. "We haven't started essay work yet, but she's a great contributor to group discussion." This is not entirely true. I said one sentence about *The Giver*, and it's because Dan asked me a direct question.

"And friends?" Melissa asks, ignoring Dan and looking only at me. "If I can think all the way back to middle school, I remember the social dynamic can be a bit . . . brutal."

I blink back at her like I have no idea what she's talking about.

"She's taking theater!" Ginger says too loudly. "Her new friend Maxwell is in most of her classes, and he's introduced her to the theater crowd. Right, Lou?"

I nod.

Melissa raises an eyebrow at me and writes something down. And then the silence stretches into minutes that feel like years.

"When can I see my mom?" I want to ask her about this SPD stuff. I want to know if any other teacher ever mentioned it and she never told me. I want to know what else she's never said.

I see Dan put an arm around Ginger.

Melissa clicks her pen. "Well, Lou, that depends on her and on you. She's got to prove herself able to support the two of you—get a steady job and a permanent living situation. If she can do that, she'll petition the court to be granted full custody again. But," she says in a way that makes me think whatever's coming next is really what she came here to say, "the judge will also ask you what you want before a final decision is made. So, you need to think on that. Would you want to stay here with your aunt and uncle, assuming they are willing to take on physical and financial responsibility? Or do you want to move back in with your mom?"

How can she ask me that? I've only been here a week. I sneak a look at Ginger. She's picking at the seam in her skirt just like I do. I have no idea what she's thinking. I have no idea what I'm thinking, other than that I want answers.

"But this was not your question," Melissa continues. "Your question was when can you *see* her, and that, really, is up to Maria and child services in California. Once they file the report on their end, we can arrange a meeting. And I promise to let you know as soon as I do when that is. Okay?"

I think I nod. I don't hear anything she says after that. It all sounds impossibly formal and complicated. Everything is so complicated. She hands Dan and Ginger a pamphlet titled, "Resources for Kinship Caregivers" on her way out.

We eat an early dinner. No one talks much. I catch Ginger eyeing the pamphlet on the kitchen counter. They invite me to watch a movie with them, one of the *Star Wars*, but I claim homework. "On a Friday night?" Dan says, but they let me go. It's been a long week for all of us.

Once I'm in my room, I turn off all the lights and curl up on the reading chair. The moonlight draws stripy patterns across my feet. I pull up Spotify on my phone. Already the iPod is "old school," as Well put it. I scroll through his "Suzy Lee playlist," because he decided I needed a soundtrack. I hit play on Lenka's "Everything's Okay." It's a beautiful song. Piano and claps and hope. I sing to myself and reach a hand down to Mom's guitar, but I don't pick it up.

I think about who I need. Is it Mom or Maria or Ginger or Dan or Melissa or Well or any of the people I've had to rely on in the past week? If I had to pick, who couldn't I live without? I rub my eyes and picture Mom in Tahoe on Amelie's couch. Has she picked up the phone and put it down again a million times like I have? Or is she just happy to be free, not missing me at all?

Something wakes me. A clink-clinking. I'd been dreaming of Tahoe, of that time when we went swimming in the cold waters of the lake. The sky was a cloudless blue, and I could smell the coffee from Joe's. We'd sprawled on the sun-warmed pier to dry off. Mom lifted her sunglasses and tucked a wet piece of hair behind my ear. "Today we are mermaids," she whispered.

Clink-clink. It chases the dream away. I sit up. My neck is stiff from falling asleep crooked against the window. There it is again. *Clink-clink.* Pause. *Clink-clink-clink.*

I check my phone. It's two a.m.

Clink.

It's coming from outside.

I scooch down in the reading chair so only my head sticks up enough to give me a view of the patio.

Clink-clink.

There's Well in the moonlight, crouched like a burglar in a black hoodie on the edge of the fire pit. I throw my sweatshirt over my pajamas and tiptoe down the stairs. The French doors aren't locked. I roll my eyes. Only in suburbia would you leave your doors unlocked. I slip out into the night.

"What are you doing here?" I whisper when I reach him, even though there's no way Ginger and Dan could hear me from the far reaches of their bedroom. Well hops down and props his feet up on a lounge chair. He's wearing glow-in-the-dark Skechers.

"I'm coming to rescue you."

"From?"

"Yourself, dearie."

"What makes you think I need rescuing?" I tuck my hands inside my sleeves. It's freezing out here. The weather changed with the rain. Was my talk with Andrea just this morning? It feels like years and years ago.

"Fine. You don't. Maybe it was just my imagination that you were basically mute today at school." I look down at my feet. Well points at the sky. "But it's a full moon and we're both up, so hang with me for a minute, will you?"

Lit up as it is by moonlight, the wet lawn looks almost like a lake. At its far end, the gate that leads to the path through the forest is just visible. Something near my foot catches my eye.

"Is that a quarter?"

Well blinks at me a second before he says, "I couldn't find any rocks."

"What?"

I bend down and follow a trail of quarters from the patio. It ends in a small pile two stories below my window.

"Is this what woke me up?" I ask.

He nods and doesn't look one bit embarrassed. This kid can *literally* throw money away.

I hold up my phone. "Why didn't you just call?"

He grins. "I saw it in a movie once."

We sit next to each other on the lounge chair. I make sure there's enough room that we aren't touching. I think back to this morning. Andrea. The SPD. It sounds fake. I glance at Well, his hair almost blue in this light. I will never tell him. I've never had a friend like Well, or any friend, really. I could blame it on moving so much, but it's not just that. Getting close to someone is hard when you can't get . . . close. If he knows there's something wrong with me, he'll act different, and I always want him to be exactly like this.

He catches me looking at him. "So?" he asks.

"So, what?"

"Are you going to try out for *Into the Woods*?"

I snort. I can't help it. The idea is snortable. "Um, no."

"Why not? It's a musical. You can sing better than miss priss Mary Katherine, who you *know* is going to get one of the leads."

Mary Katherine is an eighth grader in our class. Sometimes she rolls her uniform skirt so short you can actually see her shirttail hanging out underneath.

"Never will I ever get onstage." *Not again.*

"That's just great." He stands up and starts marching around the fire pit. *This is new,* I think. *Mad Well.* "You can sing me and Geneva under the table, and we're still trying out. Tucker is helping to build the set, which is one almighty set, because he basically has to hammer together a forest for Little Red Riding Hood, a castle for Cinderella, Rapunzel's tower, the beanstalk . . . I can't even remember what else now." He stops. "Anyway, Jacob's helping with sound *and* lights. And what are *you* going to do? Sit and knit?"

"No. I'm assistant director." I hadn't told anyone this part yet, because I wasn't sure I was going to do it.

"Oh." He stops and sits down again.

"I talked to Mrs. Nicky about it yesterday. She told me that everybody in class has to do something. So, I could either help with the costumes, be a stagehand, or, and I quote, 'assist me in directing this musical so it does not turn into a monstrosity.' When I asked her what an assistant director actually did, she said, 'Keep the menagerie in line.' Whatever that means."

"So, if I get a part," Well says, "which I will, because this cast is huge and our class is not and also because I am awesome, you're going to be bossing me around?"

"Yep."

"Huh. All right. Actually, that's excellent." He jumps up again. "Will you promise to tell Mary Katherine every single time she misses a high note?"

"I swear." I hold my hand to my heart. I guess I *am* taking the job.

"No." He turns to me and holds out his hand. *"Pinky promise."*

His nail is emerald green. He must have done that tonight. I look at it, and my heart trips over itself. I can't take it. Even this kind of small contact is too hard. It's not that I think his hands are dirty or sweaty. It's just too *unknown*, like an alien offering a high five. It could be awesome, or it could be terrible. My heart starts thumping. I push my knuckles against the fabric of the chair until I hear the threads creak. Well's still waiting, like he has all the time in the world, while I panic.

The moment stretches and stretches until it's almost like an out-of-body experience. I can see myself, sitting crisscross-applesauce, looking up at a boy who actually thinks I'm not a freak show. His hand casts a shadow across the patio. *Just do it,* I want to yell. *Just wrap your finger around his and make a promise. It's the easiest thing in the world.* But I jump to my feet instead.

"It's freezing! How'd you get here, anyway?"

Well's hand falls. And then he gives me a wicked grin. "Well, Suzy Lee, I may have 'borrowed' my dad's golf cart." I follow where he's now pointing and spot a white golf cart half in the grass, half on the sidewalk.

"You drove that all the way here?"

"It's just a few miles."

"You drove a stolen golf cart a few miles down the road in the middle of the night?"

"*Borrowed* golf cart."

I bet the police wouldn't see it that way, I think, remembering the night of the crash. If Well wrecked it and hurt himself, I wonder if his dad would get in trouble like my mom. Probably not. People with enough money to own golf carts as toys don't get investigated for neglect.

"Your dad is going to freak."

Well shrugs, his favorite gesture, and pulls the hood from his sweatshirt up so his face falls into shadow. "Nah. One"—he holds up a finger—"he'd have to notice me first to notice I'm gone. And two"—he counts off—"he'd have to be home."

"Is your mom there?"

"Nope. San Francisco—permanently. When they divorced, she moved back there to be closer to her family. In case you hadn't noticed, there's not a big Japanese-American crowd in the Bible Belt. Dad's actually from New Jersey. I don't know what kind of voodoo he pulled to get her to marry him and move here in the first place. He's *very* successful in his business, but an epic failure at the whole marriage thing. And the parenting thing."

So Well's mom is in California too. I bet she misses him. I bet she calls. I bet she flies him first class out to see her. I wonder if he wishes he could live there around people who look more like him. But if he did, we would never have met, and I already can't picture that version of my life.

"So, you're home alone?" I ask.

"Um, no. The *home* is alone. I, however, am here with the lovely Louise Montgomery, and she is about to sing me a song that will carry me safely onward."

"No, uh-uh." I move backward toward the French doors.

"Oh, come on. We can do what we did before. Just pick a song. Anything. And we'll pull it up on my phone. And I won't even look at you. Swear. We can turn back to back, and you can pretend you are allllllllll alone."

I picture him going back to his empty house. He's more alone than me right now. And I think of the pinky promise I couldn't make. I can do this, though. I can sing.

"All right," I say, despite the fact that I want to puke.

"All right!"

"Shhhh!"

"Okay, okay. What do you want to sing?"

Nothing, I want to say, while he pulls out his phone. But then something comes to me, and I tell him to put it away. I don't need the music.

"Turn around," I say, and he does so we're back to back but not touching. Then I close my eyes, and it's like I really *am* all alone, singing to myself:

I start off low and quiet, so it's almost a hum.

"'You are my sunshine, my only sunshine . . .'"

I can see Mom lying next to me in our truck bed with the canopy off so we can watch for shooting stars. This was our bedtime song. My heart twists. It *hurts* to sing it, and I wonder, wherever she is, if she feels it right now too.

"'In all my dreams, dear, you seem to leave me . . .'"

When I hear it like this, in the dark with Well, I realize it's not a lullaby at all. It's the saddest song in the world sung to the person three thousand miles away who broke my heart. After it's over, I turn around. Well has his head in his hands. Is he missing his mom too?

I tug on his hood. He looks up.

"Lou," he says, his voice pleading, "if you don't sing in this show, it'll just break my heart."

I have never wished for physical contact in my

entire life. But right now all I want to do is shove Well into the fire pit.

"Broken hearts make for great acting," I say, and jerk his hoodie closed. Now he's just two eyes peering out of a dark hole.

He mimes an arrow to the heart and falls down.

"You're killing me, Lou. You are absolutely killing me."

10
There's No Business Like Show Business

It's the end of October. The month-anniversary of my car wreck and the last time I saw my mother. The last time I *spoke* to my mother. I've called Joe hundreds more times. And hung up when he answered. What good does it do to check up on her when she's not checking up on me? Wherever she is, she's got a phone. Maybe she's decided to make Tahoe permanent, just without me. Last Saturday, I slid her guitar under my bed. There's no point keeping it tuned, so why keep it out?

It's fine though, really. I have my own life now. Ginger and Dan and I even have Taco Tuesdays. She picks up food from a place downtown near her work, and we eat in the living room, watching episodes of *Modern Family* and trying not to drop queso on the leather couches. I love Taco Tuesday.

Yesterday the weather turned warm again. So today Mrs. Nicky has taken the class outside into the golden sunlight to run lines. I'm sitting on top of a picnic table with the script in my lap. Geneva is lying on her stomach at my feet, drawing a seahorse on her arm. The green in her hair has faded to moss. She looks a little mildewed. But it's a lovely mildew.

Well is in the shade of the oak tree that grows just outside the entrance to the dining hall. That oak drops acorns on your head like tiny bombs if you're not careful. It's also got a perfect curve for your back. You can lean against it forever. These are the things I know because I've been here a month. This is what happens when you hang around a place long enough to be more than a traveler passing through.

Jacob and Tucker got a pass to study hall today,

because, as Mrs. Nicky put it, "Their services are not needed." I wish that were true for Mary Katherine, or any of the eighth graders. None of them know their lines, which means that I, as the assistant director, am basically reading the entire script aloud.

"No!" Mrs. Nicky yells, and snaps her fingers. I jump, and Geneva lifts her head. "Stop shaking the table."

"Sorry," I mumble. Even when I know it's coming, it's still hard to make my body stay still.

"Mary Katherine, Lacey, Evan . . . you three *listen* to me." Mrs. Nicky pushes up the sleeves of her shirt. It's a man's button-down, and the sleeves fall right back down over her jangly bracelets. "This is a story of *wanting*."

She starts marching around the picnic tables.

"Wanting what you can't have and giving up everything, *everything*," she stage whispers, "to get it. Rapunzel, you want freedom. Cinderella, you want love. And Jack, you're not just trying to sell a cow. You want fortune and glory. But—" She pauses and looks every one of them in the eye where they sit cross-legged in front of her. "But," she whispers again, "that is just the beginning of the story. This is about what happens *after* happily ever after."

Mrs. Nicky is good at monologuing. All three of them nod. But I can see Mary Katherine texting under her leg. Well smirks. Despite what he said about getting a small part, he's the Baker, the one who basically ties all the characters together. Geneva is the Witch, which is right up her alley. Yesterday, at lunch, she practiced casting a spell on her cheese sandwich to turn it into a grilled cheese sandwich. She said it was to get into character. She made me taste it. We both agreed it *was* a little warmer. She and Well already know their lines.

But as the assistant director, or AD, I'm looking at the production calendar and counting down the six weeks we have until the show and wondering how all these different parts and all these different people will come together to become the "musical masterpiece" that Mrs. Nicky claims it will be. I'm glad I'm going to be standing offstage on opening night.

When the bell rings at the end of class, Mrs. Nicky throws her hands up in exasperation and stalks off, leaving me to gather up all the scripts and return them to the dance room. Well helps, claiming chivalry, but I know he just doesn't want to go to English. We have an in-class essay on *The Giver* today, and he hasn't even finished the book.

"I can't believe you didn't make it through *The Giver*, but you can read and memorize this script in a week," I say, stacking the black binders up against the wall once we get to the dance room.

"*The Giver* is so *boring*," he whines.

"*The Giver* is about doing your own thing when everyone else tells you it's wrong. It's basically *about* you, for heaven's sake!"

He stops stacking binders and starts fixing his hair in the mirror. "You want to write my essay for me, then?"

"No, I do not. And that was the late bell. Come on. I may live with him, and he may like me for helping him with his crossword puzzles, but at school, Dan will definitely give me demerits."

"Fine. Then *after* I fail the essay, do you want to come over to my house with Geneva and the guys tomorrow night? We're dressing up and watching *Hocus Pocus* for Halloween."

"Okay. Yeah. Just come on." I have no idea what *Hocus Pocus* is, and in all this time Well and I have spent together, we've never been to his house, but I see Andrea in the hallway and I will do and say anything to get away.

I've gotten really good at avoiding her. I come in the back entrance to school in the morning and make a wide sweep of the front offices if I'm ever on the first floor. I know she knows I'm dodging her. I know she wants to bring up the sensory stuff again. But obviously there's nothing to talk about, because I'm fine, I'm managing it all on my own, so why talk at all?

Dan drops me off at Well's place at seven p.m. sharp. I haven't been nervous until now, because I've spent the last month getting used to Well, and he's about as close as anyone can be to making me feel comfortable. But now that I'm standing with my feet on the flagstone driveway leading up to the enormous wooden doors of his ginormous house that is all stone and wood and copper rain gutters, I can't move. Well lives in a *palace*. The front doors have actual antlers for handles. I count the garage doors—one, two, three, four—in a separate miniature version of the main house. An entire home for your cars. Imagine that. Well told me there's a pool, too. Of course there is.

What would he or Geneva or Jacob or Tucker think if they knew I was living in a truck a month ago? I have a deep craving to dive headfirst into my old sleeping bag, wherever it is three thousand miles away, and never come out again. But then Well opens the door wearing a green silk dress complete with corset, heels, and black lipstick, and I feel . . . better. Well is 100 percent a person who lives by his own rules. He wouldn't care if I lived in a hot-air balloon before this. Actually, he would love that.

After Dan beeps his horn and drives off, Well grins at me and then frowns. "You didn't dress up!"

"And you dressed up as . . . a Disney princess?"

"NO! Have you seriously never seen *Hocus Pocus*?" He shakes his head at my jeans and Hard Rock sweat-shirt and Converse. I'm really proud of my Converse.

They are bright red and the first "new" thing I let Ginger buy me that I got to pick out.

"Um, no?" I say. Should I have previewed this movie to make sure it's not loaded up with things to make me scream or jump or cry? I know my triggers. I can't believe I didn't come more prepared.

"If we're getting all honest here"—Well leans in—"neither have I. But it's Bette Midler *and* Halloweeny. If you want to be a real *thespian*, you have to watch it."

"What's a thespian again?"

"Ha. Ha. Get in here. Everybody else is already downstairs."

I follow him down the polished spiral staircase, keeping my distance, because he is clomping along in five-inch heels, and he is not very good at it. I wonder where he even got them, or the corset, for that matter.

"I raided the costume closet at school," he says, even though I didn't ask. "The high school did *Gone with the Wind* a few years ago."

When we get to the bottom of the stairs, I forget all about the dress. "You're kidding me, right?" Red velvet theater seats five rows deep sit in front of a screen that stretches all the way along the wall. There's even a curtain to pull across it.

Apparently Well's version of "come watch a movie at my house" is actually "come watch a movie in my *theater*." My stomach bottoms out at the idea of it. A whole room of your own just for movies.

"What?" He grins. He has a smudge of black lipstick on his front tooth.

"So, be real honest here. Is your dad a millionaire?"

"Honestly? Yeah. Now come on! I've got marshmallow ghosts and peanut butter pumpkins." He clomps away, but I'm still trying to take it in. Where do you *put* a million dollars? Mom and I never even had a bank account.

Geneva sees me frozen by the foot of the stairs and waves me over from the very back row (because the basement theater is big enough to have a "very back row"). I focus on my red shoes and make myself move. When I get to her, she stands to give me an air kiss. That's the thing I appreciate about Geneva. She's all air kisses and nods, no contact. I think she dislikes touching people as much as I do. Tonight she's in a black cat outfit, complete with ears and tail.

Tucker waves from down the row. He's got his size-thirteen feet up on the back of the seats in front of him. Like me, he's not dressed up, except for a black witch's hat, which I have a feeling Well forced on him. I plop down next to him, careful to keep my elbows tucked in. He burps, long and loud.

"Tuck! Ugh." Geneva turns up her nose, a perfectly irritated cat.

"Sorry! The contest was today. I'm still recovering," he says, waving the air in front of him like he can shoo away the smell.

He means the hot-dog-eating contest at the Halloween carnival. I wanted to go, but the thought of dunk tanks and balloon-popping games and creaking Ferris wheels was too much. It's all the worst things about the state fair with none of the music. Basically, the worst nightmare for someone with a sensory processing disorder. Not that I'm saying I have one.

"How'd it go?" I ask.

"It was gruesome and revolting," Geneva says, patting his shoe. "He did great."

"Yeah," Tucker says, reddening all the way up to his ears. "I got second place. Forty-two dogs. The winner got forty-five."

"Yes, but he puked after the buzzer. They should disqualify you for that," Geneva says with authority.

"It's okay. I'm happy with second. Made my mom proud. We won a twenty-five dollar gift certificate to Target."

"She wasn't grossed out?" I have to ask, because I almost just threw up from the smell of his burp.

"Nah, she loves it. One time, when I was ten, she caught me drinking one of those SlimFast shakes after school and smacked it right out of my hand."

"Why?"

"She said, 'Son, you don't mess with the body the good Lord gave you. God made you to be a man of stature. You better figure out how to use it, not lose it.'"

"I love your mom," Geneva says, pulling his hat off and trying it on. Witch cat.

"Yeah, she could probably win that hot dog contest without even trying. The woman knows her way around a buffet."

Tucker laughs, but it's sweet. I can tell he loves her. I bet she leaves the light on in the hallway for him at night and packs a note in his backpack every day. I bet she asked him where he was going tonight and when he would be home. Because those are the kinds of things mothers do. Or should do. When they're around. And acting like mothers instead of stage managers. I squeeze my armrest. Suddenly I'm ready to stop talking and start the movie.

"Are we good to go?" Jacob yells from the little closet-size room behind us where the projector is queued up and ready to play. He's also not in a costume, I notice. Unless one of the characters in the film wears jeans and a SpongeBob T-shirt.

Well hands us big bowls of candy and shouts, "Lights, camera, action!" and the screen flickers to life. I tense up and wave off the candy when Geneva passes it to me. If there are any startling noises in this movie, I will have to run out. I know this. Mom took me to a free movie in the park once. It was *Frozen*. When Elsa started turning everything to ice and the ice *craaaaaacked* over the dance floor and up the walls,

I cried so loud the families around us started whispering, and Mom had to carry me to the truck. Please don't let this be like that. I don't have a mother to carry me out of here.

But it turns out I have nothing to worry about. Whatever the opposite of sensory stimulus is, that's what this is. Sensory paralysis. Twenty minutes in, Geneva is the first one to say it.

"Guys. This movie sucks."

"What!" Well says, like she insulted his sweet old grandma.

"Come on, *Max*well. It's not even scary." She points to the screen as Billy the Zombie crawls out of a grave and roars like an angry toddler.

"And the special effects," Tucker adds. "Dude. They're terrible. The talking cat looks like a bad robot."

"I didn't want to mention this, but," Jacob says, not even pausing the game of Minecraft on his phone, "the copyright was 1993."

Well sinks down in his seat and throws a fistful of candy at Jacob. The lights from the screen draw prisms on his face. I bite into my fifth marshmallow ghost so I don't have to give an opinion. After two more minutes where we watch the robot cat get run over by a car and then reinflate like a balloon, he throws up his hands.

"Fine," Well says. "Jacob, kill the reel."

"Do you think Mrs. Nicky might actually kill Mary Katherine before opening night?" Well asks through a mouthful of pizza.

We are in the kitchen now, sitting on top of the granite countertops eating Little Caesars, which Well ordered with his dad's credit card. He moved his jack-o'-lantern inside "for ambiance" as he put it, and it's winking at us from the top of the stove. Well has loosened his corset, so now it kind of looks like a cowboy's vest.

"The real question," Geneva says, looping a string of cheese onto her finger and into her mouth, "is do you think she'll catch Mary Katherine making out with Evan in the costume closet?"

"Really?" Am I the only one who misses these things?

"Oh come on, Lou. You're telling me you haven't

noticed them texting during class?" Jacob says, which is maybe even more surprising than Mary Katherine and Evan kissing. Jacob doesn't notice anything that doesn't come pixelated on a screen.

"But they're only in eighth grade," I add. Geneva gives me one of her "did you just crawl out from under a rock" looks. My face flushes red. That's what I get for spending the last year with only Mom for company.

"Can we not talk about theater for *thirty seconds*," Jacob says now, flipping his laptop toward us. "Because this is classic."

We watch a cat hop up on a toilet, squat, do its business, and then turn around and flush. Cat videos on YouTube are another cultural gap I'm just now starting to fill in.

"Niiiiiiice," Tucker says, tipping an entire packet of Parmesan cheese in his mouth. How could anyone possibly be hungry after forty-two hot dogs?

"That's disgusting," Well says to Tucker, who laughs and then coughs out a puff of cheese dust.

We hear the front door open, followed by a slam. A second later footsteps march toward the kitchen.

"Get down. Get down off the counter!" Well whispers. "Tucker, put a coaster under that glass!"

We all slide off the counters, but then we don't know where to move, so when Well's dad rounds the corner, we are standing awkwardly in the middle of the kitchen with half-eaten slices of pizza in our hands.

"Maxwell, what is this?"

Well's dad is not what I pictured. He is tan and short and muscly in a too-tight plaid shirt and alligator boots. He looks like a country music wannabe. And nothing at all like Well. I catch a whiff of his aftershave. It smells like car freshener.

"We, uh, just ordered some pizzas, Dad."

"Not the pizzas, son. The getup." He points a finger at Well's dress and the heels he has slipped off but is still standing next to. Well tugs at the edges of the corset, like a too-small blanket. The kitchen is deafeningly silent.

"We were watching *Hocus Pocus*. It's a theater thing," he explains. But his dad is already shaking his head.

"A theater thing. I'm sure it is. I'll blame that one

on your mother. Listen, you kids got a ride home?" His phone rings then, and he doesn't wait for our answer.

I guess that is our signal to leave. We all pull out our phones to call for rides. Dan answers on the first ring. He says they're finishing dinner, and he will be over in fifteen minutes. And then he whispers, "Unless this is an emergency—then I will come now."

"Why are you whispering?" I whisper back.

"I don't know. It's only been an hour. I wanted to make sure the movie wasn't too scary, or, you know . . ." He trails off. Sweet Dan, who has learned not to use the blender or bang the kitchen cabinets or hug me on the way into school, is worried about me. Tears spring to my eyes, and I'm not even sure why. I tell him fifteen minutes is fine and hang up.

Nobody looks at Well while we wait to be picked up. Not that he'd notice, since he's looking at the floor.

I'm the last one to leave, and Well walks me to the door. He's changed into a T-shirt and sweatpants. The black lipstick is gone, but there's still a faint outline, like a bruise.

We sit on the wide stone steps and wait for Dan.

"Sorry about my dad back there."

I shrug, because what is there to say?

"He just doesn't get it . . . doesn't get me. Maybe it would have been better if they'd had more kids. Or if he'd listened to my mom and moved us all to the West Coast. But I don't know, maybe not." The wind ruffles his hair forward, and he looks younger, smaller.

"My mom doesn't get me, either."

"No?"

"No. She, uh, wishes I were more like her, I think. Louder, flashier, you know."

"Is your mom a movie star or something?"

I give a sad smile. "No. She's a waitress in Tahoe." *At least she was last time I heard,* I think. It's strange not knowing. Like holding on to a very long balloon. You know it's out there, but you can't always feel it when you tug. Sometimes I don't even know if I want to feel it. Would it be better to let go? So I can stop wondering if she misses me? I twist my hair into a knot at the base of my neck and then release it so it unfurls slowly, like Mom used to do.

"So how come you're here and she's there?" Well

doesn't look at me when he asks. He's picking at his fingernail polish. Peeling it off in green strips. Which is probably why I answer his question. We've never talked about why I'm living with Ginger and Dan.

"We didn't have a lot of money. We were, uh, just camping out by the lake when the cops found out I wasn't in school."

"You camped out every night and didn't have to go to *school?*" He stops picking at his nails. "Epic."

"Uh, yeah. Except they decided it would be better if I lived with my aunt and uncle for a while." *For a while,* I think. *Whatever that means.* It's like when grown-ups say *we'll talk about it later* or *we'll be there soon.* It's an answer, but it's not. Maybe it's better Mom doesn't call, better than giving me nonanswers.

"At least it sounds like your mom was around."

I don't say anything. *Was* around. I think of this house. The four-car garage. The pool. The *movie theater.* And then I think of Well's dad, standing in the kitchen in his alligator boots in front of his son, but staring at his phone. I guess there are different kinds of neglect.

"What does your dad do, anyway?" I ask.

"He's a music producer," Well says, sounding both bored and disappointed.

I shiver, remembering Howie and the meeting we never had. Mom would jump at the chance to meet Well's dad. Good thing he's always gone, because I will not *ever* let him hear me sing.

We sit for a while, not talking. When the lights from Dan's Jeep swing around the circular drive, Well stands and holds out a hand to me, but I'm already halfway up and he lets it fall.

"I guess you can't pick family, huh?" he says, and goes inside without waving good-bye.

Ginger is in my bedroom when I get home. Which is weird. She's just sitting on the bed in her fuzzy robe and slippers.

"How was movie night?" she asks. Her voice is high, like it was the first night they picked me up from the airport.

"Okay, I guess. We didn't finish the movie."

"Oh, well, maybe next time?"

I nod. She looks strange, fidgety. She keeps tugging at the tie on her robe. I'm still thinking about Well, and I just want to be alone.

"Um, I guess I'm going to get ready for bed." I start to walk into the bathroom, thinking maybe she'll take the hint and go, but she calls after me.

"Lou, wait. Come sit down." She pats the bed beside her. I walk over to the reading chair instead.

"Lou, I found your earbuds in the laundry room, and I was just putting them away—" She leans over, and, before she can even open the top drawer of the nightstand, my face begins to burn. Shame crawls up my spine, like a spider. I tuck myself farther back in the chair.

She begins pulling out half-opened sleeves of Ritz crackers. A Twix. An unopened bag of Fritos. A chocolate chip cookie from school wrapped up in napkins. Three packages of pink-iced animal crackers. Laid out on the bed like that it looks like a lot more than it did when it was shoved in the drawer. I want to throw a blanket over it all.

"I really just want to go to bed."

"Lou, we need to talk about this." She stands and walks closer to me.

"Talk about what?" I curl away from her toward the window.

"Honey, why is all this in your room? Are you not getting enough to eat? I don't want you to feel like you have to hide food." She kneels in front of me, and I'm staring at the top of her head. "Lou, I will buy you whatever you need." She starts to put a hand out toward my knee, and I jerk away so hard my leg knocks into the window with a crack. We sit like that for a few minutes. Frozen.

I try to think of a way to explain it, but I can't. How do you explain to someone who's never gone without food for more than a couple of hours what it's like to be hungry for months? To always be looking at the leftovers on strangers' plates? To feel that gnawing in your belly and then, eventually, not to feel it at all?

"I'll take the stuff downstairs."

"No, honey. It's okay." She wipes a finger under one eye, and I can't tell if she's crying. "Keep it if you want to. I just want to know if you're okay?"

Am I okay? I don't know. How can anybody really answer that?

She sits back on her heels now, tucking her robe underneath her.

"You know, your mom and I used to sneak boxes of Ritz crackers back to our room and dip them straight into the peanut butter jar. It drove our mama crazy . . . all those crumbs."

"Mom and I do that too. With the peanut butter."

She smiles and leans her head on the leg of the chair. I look at her hands folded in her lap; the freckles reach all the way down to her fingertips. It reminds me of something.

"Ginger?"

"Hmm?"

"Did we go to a strawberry patch when I was little?"

She lifts her head and looks at me.

"I can't believe you remember that. You must have been four, maybe five. Yes, we did. Just outside of Lexington. I was finishing up law school at the University of Kentucky, and you and your mom came to visit."

"I fell in the dirt and you helped me up."

"Did I?"

"Yeah." I can feel it. The warm dirt. Starting to cry, but knowing I wasn't supposed to, because Mom told me I was a big girl now, too big to cry. And then Ginger put her hands under my arms and scooped me up. And I screamed louder. Even then I didn't like other people touching me. But then she handed me a strawberry. She was the one who handed me the strawberry, not Mom.

"Ginger, how come that's the last time I remember you?"

"Oh, honey. It's a long story."

I give her a sideways glance.

"All right." She sighs. "Did you know your mom was a volleyball player? She was brilliant, actually. She had that long, lean thing going for her, and no one had to tell *her* to be aggressive. She had scouts at her matches even in her junior year."

I didn't know any of this, because Mom never told me anything about anything past yesterday. But I can so picture it. Mom in spandex and a ponytail yelling "Spike!" and slamming the ball.

"So, what happened?" I ask, but Ginger is quiet. "Oh. Me . . . I happened." There it is, the real reason Mom's not calling. I interrupted her life, and she's getting it back on track now. A hard lump lodges itself in my throat, even though I told myself we were both better off now. I still miss her. It's not fair how much I miss her.

"Oh, honey," Ginger says again, reading my face. "Your mom, from the *very beginning*, was so excited about you. She'd always wanted to be a mom. She would carry around old Barbies and baby them, all the way up until she was thirteen. I was the first one she told when she found out she was expecting. Did you know that? She was already pretty far along when she figured it out, but she told me first. It was spring of my sophomore year at the community college in Arkansas, and she just pulls up in front of the dorms in our parents' busted-up Pontiac and yells my name until someone tells her which room I'm in. Then she comes running in waving that pregnancy test around." Ginger laughs. "I told her to hold off on telling our parents. See if I couldn't patch things up over the summer and then we could tell them together, but I guess she just couldn't wait."

"And they weren't as excited as she was."

Ginger sighs. "Your grandparents are very hard-minded people. Slip too low or too high on the ladder and you're out. We Montgomery girls 'just didn't know our place,' as they liked to say."

"So what happened? I get why you don't talk to your parents, but how come you and Mom didn't stay close?"

Ginger runs a hand through her hair and snaps at the hair tie around her wrist.

"Your mom moved out of our parent's house, but she didn't leave town right away. She floated around with friends. After you were born, she got a job cleaning rich people's houses. They let her bring you along. You loved it—all the clients' kids' toys and Elmo on the big flat screens."

I don't remember any of this. But I can picture this, too. Mom at eighteen, nineteen, twenty, cleaning toilets and folding neat corners into bedsheets while I stack other kids' Legos.

"I was just about to graduate law school when we met up at that farm to pick strawberries. Jill and I had talked about moving in together. I'd already interned at the law firm here in Nashville, and I knew they'd offer me a job. All I had to do was pass the bar exam."

"But?"

"*But* I made a mistake. I offered your mom some money. I had a little savings, and I knew there'd be more coming my way. So I said I could pay her share of the rent and help with her tuition if she wanted to start taking some community-college classes somewhere."

I lived with Mom for twelve years. Ginger doesn't need to tell me what happened next.

"She got mad," I say.

"She got mad."

"Because you were giving her a 'handout.'"

"Yes."

This was my mom. She'd take a free sandwich from Joe's after a show with a "please and thank you," but try to give her "charity" and she'd just as soon spit in your eye. It had to be some kind of trade or nothing at all. There was a lady once, in Biloxi, the mom of a girl from my class. I guess she noticed my raggedy jeans and the hole in my Keds. Or maybe it was that I wore the same striped T-shirt almost every day. Anyway, she brought a whole bag of clothes to school for me. Skirts from the Gap and collared shirts from H&M already soft from washing. There was a whole pile of shoes, too. But when Mom caught me trying them on in our motel room that night, she made me pack every single thing back up and return it the next day. I cried all the way to school with the bag sitting next to me on the bus.

"Did you ever try to see her again?" I ask Ginger. And by "her" I really mean "me."

"Oh, Lou, *of course* I did. But she just . . . disappeared. No forwarding address. No phone number. Nothing. Apart from the occasional postcard, she was off the map. Honey—" Her voice breaks. "I'm so sorry. I'm so sorry I am just now getting to know you."

She's for-real crying now, and so am I. But I'm more angry than sad. I'm mad at Mom for keeping every important detail from me. What my grandparents were really like. The fact that my aunt was a lawyer and nice and *wanted to see me*. Even the volleyball and that she used to clean people's houses. If our past is part of what makes us who we are, like she said *every time* we had to move, then she hid 90 percent of herself from me.

I've never cried with someone. It's always been me alone, in the truck or hospital room or airport or this very bedroom. It feels kind of good to cry with Ginger. I give in to it another minute and then stand up and go over to the bed. I scoop up all the crackers and candy and cookies and drop them in Ginger's lap.

"Lou, you can keep these," Ginger says, cradling the pile in her arms like a baby. "How about this: We can put them on your bookshelf so you don't feel like you have to hide them?"

"No, you take them."

"Are you sure?"

"Yeah. I know where they'll be if I need them." I smile at her because I mean it.

"Okay." She stands up uncertainly. "Well, good night, honey."

She wants to hug me so much. I can see it. I kind of want to hug her, too, to lean into someone instead of myself, but that doesn't mean my body will agree. I know it too well for that. So I take a step back as she takes one forward. It's the saddest kind of slow dance. She smiles anyway and then quietly shuts the door on her way out.

I lie on the bed and think about what Well said, about how you can't pick family. Then I think about Ginger and Dan downstairs probably brushing their teeth in their side-by-side sinks. Well's wrong. Maybe you can't pick who you get in the beginning, but you can *sure* pick who you end up with.

11
On the Road to Nowhere

W e're on a road to nowhere,'" Alexa booms over and over from the piano bench. I bob my head and hum under my breath.

"Mrs. Nicky? What *is* this?" Mary Katherine shouts over the refrain. Next to me, Well sighs. She is the ruiner of all good things.

"Alexa, stop," Mrs. Nicky orders wearily. "Mary Katherine, *this* is the Talking Heads, and I have deep misgivings about your generation if you know every Miley Cyrus song but you don't know the Talking Heads."

"My mom won't let me listen to Miley Cyrus."

"That's one point to your mom, Jacob."

"Do you *want* to listen to Miley Cyrus, Jacob?"

"Shut up, Tucker."

"All of you, listen. You know I despise demerits and the entire negative reinforcement system, *but* I will pass them around like licorice if we do *not* stay on task today, because this show is in one month. ONE MONTH. And we don't have a moment to lose. Sooooo," Mrs. Nicky drags out, "why do you think I played this song today?"

"Because you want us to be depressed?" Mary Katherine says.

"Because we forgot our lines again and you're punishing us?" Evan adds, and moves an inch closer to Mary Katherine so they are basically overlapping.

"No! No, people. I played this song because *this* is what the opening of act 2 is all about. The Baker's finally got himself a son."

Well takes a little bow here.

"And Jack is rich and Cinderella's married her prince," Mrs. Nicky continues.

"But . . . ," Geneva says from her spot by the mirrors, because she loves getting Mrs. Nicky on a roll.

"*But* all is not perfect in fairy-tale land. The Baker and his wife bicker. Jack misses the beanstalk world. Cinderella's Prince is less than charming. And so we watch and we wait"—she starts pacing the room now like a jungle cat in spangly bracelets—"for our heroes to learn their lesson. Which is?"

Everybody finds a spot on the wall or the floor. Something to stare at so they don't have to speak.

Mrs. Nicky grabs the demerit slips. I can't believe I'm doing it, but I raise my hand.

"Yes, Lou?"

"The story doesn't end when we get what we want."

"Speak up, dear. Be a tigress, not a mouse!"

"The story's not over when we get what we want!" I yell, and Geneva applauds and I only flinch a little.

"Yes!" Mrs. Nicky cheers, throwing the pack of demerit slips like a Frisbee so they go sailing under the piano bench. "Listen to your assistant director, people. We cannot stop growing. *Learn* from your mistakes and move, move, move onward!"

As Mary Katherine rolls her eyes, Well leans over and whispers in my ear, "I think that was her round-about way of telling the eighth graders they better learn their lines or else."

Dan's classroom is exactly how you would picture an English room at a fancy private school. Three walls are covered floor to ceiling in bookshelves, with gaps like big white teeth for the dry-erase and Smart boards. The last wall isn't a wall. It's one big window overlooking the faculty parking lot and the hills beyond. There are four photographs of the very same hills hung above the window, one taken in each season of the year. This way, he says, when you're dead stuck in the middle of winter, you can look up and see spring just around the corner.

I'm staring at the picture of spring, with tiny bright green buds dusting the trees like pollen, when class starts. I'm worn out from my small bit of participation in theater class today. I can't believe I shared the "moral of the story," as Mrs. Nicky calls it, with the class. I'm a little proud, too, though. I want to tell Andrea so she will stop leaving notes in my locker with the names of occupational therapists. But first, all I want to do is sink down in my seat in the back row and take this period off. That's how I've learned to do it. If one class is a little too intense, a group dissection in science or a debate where everyone's yelling in history, then whatever class comes next, I just . . . check out. I don't sleep or anything. I just sit there with my eyes open and let my mind drift.

"Psst. Pssssssssst," Well whispers next to me. He does *not* understand the concept of taking a period off.

"What?"

"Coach is passing back the essays."

"And?"

"And you're going to have to hold my hand if I failed."

I shake my head as Dan walks up and down the rows, a stack of papers in his hand. Well is always trying to get me to hold hands, high-five, pinky-swear, fist-bump. I never do it.

Dan is just turning down the aisle farthest from me when it happens. Later, I think maybe if he had been a little closer, it wouldn't have played out like it did. But then again, probably not. Some things are inevitable, like a train running on a broken track. Eventually it's going to crash.

My train wreck is the fire alarm in fifth-period English.

It screams. I grab my ears and then my hair. It's not stopping. I pull at my hair. Harder. Harder. Until some comes away in my hands. The pain helps. But not enough.

Through my arms I see people standing, laughing, texting. They are walking out. I begin to rock in my seat. Still the alarm wails. Well sticks his face in front of mine. He's saying something, but I can't hear him over the siren and my own fast breathing. Then he grabs at my arm. I scream and jerk away. The last ones in the room turn to watch. They're watching me, the freak.

I don't care. I don't care about anything right now but noise. I can feel it, burrowing in my ears like a worm. I'll never get it out. Make it stop. I'm on the floor. How did I get here? Now I'm in someone's arms. Make them stop. Too much touching. Too much sound. I'm being carried down the hall, out into the cold, cold air. And suddenly, finally, it is quiet.

The grass is wet by the tree where I lie. It seeps into my skirt. Dan is on his hands and knees in front of me. He carried me here. Not from a fire. From a fire *drill*. I look past his shoulder. Kids talk and laugh in lines snaking across the parking lot. This is their idea of fun. A break from class. Principal Myers blows a whistle. They all begin to wander back inside. But not before glancing at me, the girl on the ground with pieces of her hair in her hands. I duck my head into the grass and pretend I am far, far away.

I do not go to school for the remaining three days before Thanksgiving break. I do not go to rehearsal. I do not answer Well's texts. I do not listen to music or look at Mom's guitar, which is still shoved under my bed. I do not let Ginger make me an appointment with Andrea. I shower. I eat. I rub antibiotic on the places in my scalp that are raw where I tore away my own hair.

We leave for the beach Wednesday morning. This

is what Ginger and Dan do every Thanksgiving. They drive to Seaside, Florida, and stay in a condo and eat seafood instead of turkey to give their thanks. I don't really care what we do. I don't care about much of anything. I lean up against the window in the backseat of the Lexus and watch the world slip away.

It takes seven and a half hours to get to the ocean. Somewhere on the Alabama highway, Ginger twists around in her seat and lifts her sunglasses to look at me.

"There's something we need to talk about."

There's a red barn with SEE ROCK CITY painted on it. I follow it with my eyes until it's out of sight.

"I don't want to talk about what happened at school," I say after it passes.

"It isn't that."

"What, then?"

She twists some more in her seat to get another inch closer to me, and Dan reaches out to turn down the audio book. It's some Tom Clancy mystery he picked up at Cracker Barrel on the way out of town. He called it his "beach read."

"It's about your mom," Ginger says.

Something in my chest stirs. It's fear raising its head.

"What? What's happened to her?"

"Nothing's happened. It's good news!" Ginger's voice is doing that thing again, fake cheery and two octaves too high, her Mary Poppins voice. "She's coming to Nashville. Melissa called yesterday to let me know she's requested a visit. Isn't that great?"

Mom. In Nashville.

"Why didn't she just call you?" *Or me?*

A pause hangs heavy in the air before Ginger speaks.

"Until we have the hearing and the court makes its decision on custody, it has to be a supervised visit. I'm sure she was just trying to play it straight."

Play it straight. Yeah, right. When has Mom *ever* played it straight? We used to sneak into chain hotels for free breakfast. No one ever looked twice at the mother and daughter at the waffle station as long as we were mostly clean. Even at the casinos, she was always looking for an angle. She lied about my age to get me into those karaoke nights. I look out the window. Pine trees and dirt and a warped sign letting the world know there's a McDonald's and a Hardee's at the next exit.

"When?"

"Next week, after we get back. If that's okay with you?"

I don't say anything. Eventually Ginger turns back around. When has anybody cared about what's okay with me?

The condo is on the bottom floor of a towering complex the deep pink color of salmon. It overlooks the ocean. And then, as if that's not enough, there's a pool about a hundred yards away. This is not beer cans and cigarette butts in the sand next to a broken grill. This is rented umbrellas and daiquiris from the poolside bar. This is how rich people do the beach.

Our first night here, we pick up fried fish sandwiches and hush puppies from a place next to an outdoor market selling sundresses and straw hats. We take them back to the condo and eat around the glass dining table. Afterward, Dan digs in the cupboard underneath the bar area and pulls out battered games of Monopoly and Boggle.

"Want to play?" he asks me. He looks so hopeful

with his bare feet on the tile floor. I shake my head.

"I will dominate you in Boggle," Ginger says to him, still false cheery. They are playing their parts, but I don't want to play mine. I'm too tired to pretend to care.

She shows me to my room. The bed is white wicker, and there's a sliding glass door that leads out to my own patio. I can hear Dan shaking the Boggle box in the living room. I turn off the lights, slide open the door, and lie down on the bed so I can hear the ocean. The rolling in and out of the waves is nice, a noise that my stupid body has decided is safe.

If I could figure out why waves are calming but fire alarms are terrifying, would it make a difference? Could I be normal then? But what if there *are* no reasons? What if this is just who I am, forever and ever? Forget friends. Forget school. Forget plays and movie nights and midnight talks with Well. Maybe Mom was onto something. Maybe we were better off alone.

It's Thanksgiving Day. Ginger, Dan, and I are sitting at a table on the top-floor open deck of a restaurant called Bud and Alley's. It's cool up here with the wind blowing. Heaters have been placed around all the tables, and I scoot as close as I can to the metal coils without getting burned. Jimmy Buffett's "Margaritaville" is playing over the loudspeakers when the waitress brings out our tray of fish tacos and fried squid. This isn't the weirdest way I've spent Thanksgiving. One year Mom had me singing outside the doors of a Best Buy at midnight to hit up the Black Friday shoppers. We took in a good haul. Folks had a lot of money to burn. But I don't want to think about Mom right now, or anything really. I focus on my food instead.

I'm squeezing lemon on my fish when Dan raises his hand like he's in class. "Why don't we go around and say what we're thankful for this year?" He's wearing a gray cardigan over a Hawaiian shirt and his nose is a painful sunburned red. He is the nerdiest, most earnest person I know. It's a shame I'm going to have to quit his class because I'm too much of a freak to be in school.

"Fine. I'll start," he says when neither Ginger nor I speak. "I am thankful for coffee in the morning, crossword puzzles in pen, a newly strung tennis racket, a beautiful wife, and a brilliant niece who got an A on her English essay."

"Thanks for putting me *after* the tennis racket," Ginger says through a mouthful of crab. "All right, my turn. I'm thankful I don't have to wear heels for five days, for a husband who can reach the top shelf in the pantry, for mocha fudge chunk ice cream, and a niece who reminds me to be brave."

They look at me, waiting for my thanks. The problem with filling your life with people is that they expect things from you, things like love and gratitude and normalcy. I pick at the skin around my thumb. "Um . . . I'm thankful for you guys and for the tacos."

They smile. Dan makes a toast to "the holidays" with his water glass and we eat and it's fine. It's really, really fine.

It's Saturday night. Ginger took me shopping at the outlet mall today. We walked through J. Crew and American Eagle and bought walnut fudge at the chocolate shop. I got a North Face jacket for 75 percent off. It was still too expensive, but Ginger insisted.

The shopping was her shot at trying to cheer me up.

They're back at the condo now playing Monopoly. I wouldn't have guessed how serious Dan gets with the board games. Last night he had to walk away from Boggle when Ginger threatened to tear up the score cards if he didn't calm down. They both seemed mostly back to normal tonight, less fake happy and more relaxed. But then, after I went to bed, I heard Dan bring up the occupational therapist that Andrea recommended. Ginger said, "I know she needs to see someone. We just can't push her yet," before they both fell into silence. So not entirely back to normal, then.

I snuck out with a blanket to sit by the ocean so I wouldn't have to hear more. It's almost dark, but not quite, and the beach is empty. I pick at one of the scabs on my head. It's beginning to flake off, settling on the shoulders of my jacket like dandruff. Perfect. I think about Monday and school. I haven't told Dan and Ginger I'm not going back. Will Well and Geneva and Tucker and Jacob, my first real friends, even notice when I'm not there? Or maybe they weren't ever really my friends. Maybe you can't be friends with someone you don't really know.

And then there's Mom, who I'm going to have to see after almost eight weeks of nothing. I wonder if she even wants to see me. Or is this just one of the steps she has to go through to give up custody? I pick at the threads of the blanket and ignore the twist my heart makes at the thought. At least I can give her back her guitar. One less reminder of her after she's gone.

My phone buzzes in the pocket of my new jacket, and when I pull it out, the screen lights up.

fine

u don't have 2 talk 2 me

but u have 2 listen 2 this . . .

It's Well. I watch the little dots hover on the screen while he types. And then he sends me a link. It's a new Spotify playlist.

LOU'S SURVIVAL PLAYLIST
"Have It All," Jason Mraz
"Unsteady," X Ambassadors
"Count on Me," Bruno Mars
"Stubborn Love," The Lumineers
"Wild Hearts Can't Be Broken," Pink

"Say Something," Justin Timberlake
featuring Chris Stapleton
"Lean on Me," Bill Withers
"Roar," Katy Perry
"Washed by the Water," Will Hoge
"Best Day of My Life," American Authors
"Imagine," John Lennon
"Don't Stop Believin'," Journey
"Awake My Soul," Mumford & Sons
"A Million Dreams," *The Greatest Showman* soundtrack
"Livin' on a Prayer," Bon Jovi
"Everything's Okay," Lenka
"We're Going to Be Friends," The White Stripes

My phone beeps with another text. It's Well again: U don't get 2 give up yet, Suzy Lee. I let my finger hover for just a second. And then I hit play.

12

All I Want for Christmas Is You

It snowed in Nashville while we were gone. We drove up late last night to a blanket of white over the bushes and the roofs. Everything looks iced in sugar. And now I'm sitting in Andrea's office waiting while she fetches tea. I decided to come back. I called Well after listening to his playlist, and he talked me into giving it one more shot. Well could talk anyone into anything. He also convinced me to talk to Andrea. "Feel your feelings, Lou," is his new mantra for me. It's annoying, but effective.

Except now that I'm here, it all feels different. Like the world I came back to is not the one I left.

"Here you go, Lou. I hope chamomile's okay."

I take a sip. It reminds me of Tahoe and Joe. In her white turtleneck with her hair tied up in a silvery scarf, Andrea looks like a winter fairy. She's waiting for me to speak. I'm the one who requested this meeting. But I don't know where to start.

"The fire drill. I know it was . . . traumatic." She's trying to get me going. But this is not the right road.

"I don't want talk about that."

"Okay." She puts down her tea. "What do you want to talk about?"

"I want to talk about the sensory processing stuff. I want to hear your plan."

"Oh, well, let me just—" I've frazzled her. She's been trying to get me to talk about this forever. Now I'm the one bringing it up. To her credit, she stands and starts rifling through her file cabinet without mentioning that I've been avoiding her like the plague for weeks. She pulls out the Adolescent Sensory Questionnaire and hands it back to me. I force myself to look at it. All the boxes I checked and all the ones I didn't that I probably should have.

She uncaps a red pen and begins to circle different

questions. She seems excited, the kind of excited adults get when they're cutting coupons or doing sudoku.

"These . . ." She points to *bothered by "light touch,"* *someone lightly touching your hand, face, leg, or back* and *distressed by others touching you.* "These indicate sensory issues related to touch."

Duh.

Now she picks up a green pen. "And these"—she circles *bothered by noises other people do not seem bothered by, sensitive to loud sounds or commotion,* and *avoid crowds and plan errands at times when there will be fewer people*—"are related to sound and crowds."

I look at the page. There is hardly anything left that *isn't* covered in red or green. She sees the look on my face.

"This is good, Lou. We know your triggers—touch and sound. There are people with additional sensory issues related to taste and textures of food, light, the whole gamut. This is manageable. That's what I'm trying to show you."

I'm not so sure. It obviously hasn't been manageable so far. "So, what now?" I ask.

"Now we get you an appointment with an OT sometime in the future to work on developing a sensory diet."

This must be the person Dan was telling Ginger about.

"What, like vitamins?"

"Not quite," she laughs. "A sensory diet involves exposing you to certain triggers, but in a *safe* environment. It helps you develop strategies to cope."

She's got to be kidding. That sounds terrible, like volunteering to get an extra flu shot.

She keeps going. "I have a few we can work on today if you like? Can I try something?" She's too eager. She holds out her hand, and I jerk back. She puts it down again. "Lou, I promise I will not lay a hand on you without your permission. Do you understand?"

I nod, but I don't scoot forward again.

"Lou, I am going to put my right hand firmly on your left shoulder for five seconds. You can count with me or count in your head. Is that okay?"

I shake my head no but then say yes before I can think more about it. I channel Well and get ready to *feel my feelings* as she puts her hand firmly on my shoulder.

"One, two, three," she counts, and my whole arm

feels like it's seizing up, like I've stuck my finger in a socket. "Four . . ." This is torture, torture disguised as therapy. "Five!" she says, and takes it away. "There. See. You did it!"

"Yeah." *But I just stood here like a cyborg and now I'm exhausted and my arm is tingly and how is this worth celebrating?* I think.

"Lou, I know you think this wasn't a big deal," Andrea says. "But it was. A lot of people do well with specific parameters like this where they know what's coming. And also, the pressure matters. Soft touch is often harder than a firm handshake or a high five."

"What about the noise?"

"That's another thing that does better with warning. A little advance notice goes a long way."

I think about the fire drill. "What if I don't get advance notice?"

Andrea gets up again and walks behind her desk to pull something out of her top drawer.

"That's what these are for." She places two purple foam earplugs on the table. They look like mutant caterpillars.

"You want me to wear earplugs?"

"Well no, not all the time. But if you keep them with you, you can use them when you hear a triggering noise. It might help stop the downward spiral. They also make noise-canceling headphones, but I thought these were a little more discreet."

I take the earplugs and put them in my pocket. I cannot imagine a scenario where I will ever let people see me using them.

"Lou, I know this all seems a little silly, but give it a shot. What can it hurt? Let's get you in with the OT I know, and we can write up a plan. And if it seems reasonable to you, we can share it with your teachers. I promise they will be sensitive and will not divulge this information to anyone."

I look into my teacup. No answers there. But I can't keep running away from my problems. I won't be like Mom.

"Okay," I whisper.

"Okay?"

"Yeah, okay. I'll try."

* * *

Well is waiting for me outside math class just like on my first day. His nails are a deep plum color. I grin. It's hard not to like a guy who makes you a playlist.

That is, until he holds up a sign that says *APPLAUSE!* in capital letters.

"*What* is that?"

"This is me, clapping loudly for your prodigal return. Get it?" He waves it around.

"Ha-ha."

Well isn't the one I'm worried about. He gets what it's like to be an outsider. His dad treats him like that every day. It's the thought of everybody else that makes me want to hide. I take a deep breath and order my feet to move.

Math and geography go exactly the same. No one looks at me, but I can feel them *wanting* to look at me. I stare at my desk, fiddling with the purple earplugs in my pocket. At lunch, I convince Well to buy snacks from the vending machine so we can skip the dining hall. I need a break from all the "not staring." We sit in the empty stairwell and look out at the snow. Another half inch and we would have gotten a snow day. I could still be in my pajamas right now.

"I don't know if I can do it," I say.

"Do what?" he asks through a mouthful of Cheetos.

"Go to theater class. Mrs. Nicky told me on my first day that theater wasn't for the faint of heart. The show's in three weeks, and I missed two rehearsals. She's going to think I can't handle the pressure."

"*Can* you?" He points a plum nail at me. The thing about Well is he doesn't ever let you off the hook.

"Yes. I mean, I think so."

"Fine." He shrugs. "Then don't let anyone bully you."

"Besides you, you mean?"

"Well of course, besides me."

Mary Katherine is the first one to openly stare. I walk in behind Well and Tucker. Jacob gives me a wave without looking up from his computer, and Geneva winks and holds out her arm. She's written *Louise* in cursive under a rabbit doing a one-armed push-up. But Mary Katherine pokes Evan in the ribs, and they both stare. For an eternity. It's like that game where you try not to blink first, except I would be happy to lose if they'd let me. Finally, Well sees it and says, "Whatchu lookin' at?" in his best Jersey accent. They roll their eyes, but at least it gets them to stop staring.

My pulse is high and fast when Mrs. Nicky marches in. I'm worried she's going to pull me aside in front of everyone. But she just launches straight into her pre-production speech of the day, giving me a quick wink as she begins.

"Three weeks, people. *Three weeks.* And we are going to need a miracle beyond fairy-tale proportions to get us show-ready in that amount of time. Lou, pass out the scripts with the stage directions we were working on before the Thanksgiving holiday so rudely interrupted our schedule." I start passing the black binders around the room. "And if one of you, just *one* of you, flubs a line that reveals you are not, in fact, off book, and you have *not* memorized your lines completely and to perfection, I'll have a fifth grader recruited in your place. Is that understood?"

Everybody says, "Yes, Mrs. Nicky," and for once today, nobody is thinking about me. Then Mrs. Nicky takes up her own binder, and that's that.

"Aren't you freezing?"

It's the end of the week, and Well and I are sitting on the curb out in front of school, waiting for Dan to pull the bus around for the boys' last tennis match of the season. Well is in the gray shiny T-shirt and navy shorts that are the tennis team's uniform. He also has a neon-green knit cap with googly eyes pulled down over his ears.

"Of course I'm cold. And more to the point, why, for the *love*, are we still playing in *December*? Tennis is a fall sport. Fall. Golden leaves and mellow sunshine. Not snow. Surely you should call a match for *snow*?"

"Aren't they indoor courts?"

"That is *not* the point. The point is that I'm telling my dad I'm quitting next year. What?" He reads the doubt on my face. "You don't think I will? I'm doing it tonight. Three-second, firm-pressure pinky promise."

This is Well's new thing. I made the mistake of telling him Andrea's coping strategies.

"No."

"Yes."

226

"No."

"It'll be good for you, and it will bring me luck."

I roll my eyes but take off one mitten. Mittens are one of the reasons I love winter. More outerwear equals less physical contact. Normally. Unless you are Well, and then nothing will stop you.

"Two seconds," I say.

"Fine."

I take his *freezing* pinky in mine and shake *one, two* times without breathing.

"Happy?" I say, pulling away. It's not *so* terrible when I know it's coming. Which I guess makes Andrea right, which is incredibly annoying.

"Happy," he says as the bus pulls up and the doors shoot open before it even comes to a full stop.

"Hurry up, kid! We're late," Dan yells, and Well hops onto the first step. He has just enough time to shout, "And good luck with your thing!" before Dan waves at me and pulls away. My thing. My meeting with my mom. Who I haven't seen in two months. Who is probably only here because the court is making her. Yes, my thing. I gulp the dry, cold air. I'm

227

going to need all the luck I can get. I spot Ginger's Lexus winding down the magnolia drive.

Here we go.

The Good Cup is a small, out-of-the-way coffee shop that Well and I have gone to before to work on our English papers. It's always almost empty, but today there's a crowd. I've never *seen* so many people here before. The shop next door is having a holiday open house. Great. More people. More noise. More of all the things I *didn't* want to manage today while also managing my mother. Ginger circles the small gravel lot, searching for a parking place in all the madness.

I picked this place because Melissa told me to choose a "neutral spot" and because the first time I came here and saw the walls lined with coffee beans, it reminded me of Bagels and Joe. But it looks like everybody in the world is trying to find a neutral spot today.

We are half an hour early, which was also my idea. Andrea says the sensory stuff is harder to manage in unexpected and/or high stress situations. I already knew this would be high stress, so I figured we could show up early, stake out the place, pick a table in the quietest corner, and get rid of as much of the "unexpected" as we could.

Once we're inside, Ginger pushes her way to the back of the line while I make a wide loop of the room and find two tiny round tables toward the back. I sit. I tuck my mittens into my pockets and hug Mom's guitar in its case between my knees. I haven't touched it in weeks. But this morning, against my better judgment, I pulled it out and tuned it. It was like meeting an old friend again.

It's been two months since I saw Mom. *Two months.* Before that I hadn't gone a day without her. I tuck my hair behind my ears. I got it cut, just a little. I catch myself hoping she'll like it. But that's stupid. Because if she cared about me at all she would have shown up or picked up the phone *at least*. She doesn't get to have an opinion about my hair.

"Have a Holly Jolly Christmas" is playing on the overhead speakers. It was already too loud, and now someone just turned it up. I squish the purple earplugs in my pocket over and over again and try to get used to the noise. I check the line. Ginger is only halfway up. My stomach rolls.

Getting here early was supposed to make me calm, but the wait is killing me. I look toward the bright red exit sign over the door, like the fixed point they tell you to find on a boat when you're seasick. Mom loves to make an entrance, but she's always been better at exits, hasn't she? Leaving my grandparents. Leaving Biloxi and all the other towns over the last twelve years. She's always leaving. I wonder how she'll do with this. I told myself I shouldn't care. So why can't I stop looking at the door?

After a thousand years, or maybe ten minutes, Ginger makes her way back through the crowd with two giant gingerbread lattes and a plate of vanilla scones. The front door jingles, and I catch sight of Melissa's dark head in the open doorway. Then I look down again. I'm not ready. I'm not.

"It's going to be fine," Ginger whispers. This is another thing adults say when they don't have the answer.

"Good, you found us a spot," Melissa says when

she reaches us, tucking her motorcycle helmet under her arm and rapping her knuckles on the table. It wobbles, and a tiny wave of my latte slurps out. All the adults look around for napkins they don't have. Then a hand reaches forward with a crumpled tissue.

"Here. This ought to do it." It's her hand and her nails, long and painted red. There's a glittery snowman on her pinky nail. She always did do a good job on her nails. More careful with them than she was with me. A sliver of anger shoots up my spine, and I straighten up to look at her.

"Hi, Lou."

I open and shut my mouth like a fish. Here she is. Right in front of me. It's her, but it's not her. She looks different. Thinner—so thin her collarbones poke out at sharp angles. A couple of inches of dark roots show in her hair. I guess she hasn't bleached it in a while. Or maybe she's stopped. Maybe that's two months of time marked right there. And her denim jacket, the one with the fake rhinestones along the collar, looks dirty and not warm enough for the weather.

And then something clicks as my heart hammers

away. She doesn't look different at all. She looks exactly like she always did. I've just never been away long enough to see her like a stranger would.

"Hi, Mom." When my voice cracks on "Mom," she looks down. Her eyes settle on my cup, and she points.

"That's a fancy coffee you got there, baby girl." I can see her adding up the price in her head, and I want to shake her. She will *not* make me feel guilty for this.

"Can I get you anything, Jill?" Ginger steps forward for the first time and looks, if possible, more nervous than me.

"Ginger." The way Mom says her name seems kind of mean. But I'm not sure how. She doesn't answer Ginger's question.

Nobody knows what to do now. We shuffle from foot to foot in our sad little triangle. When the song switches over to Mariah Carey's "All I Want for Christmas is You," Melissa steps in, breaking up the silence.

"Ginger, why don't you and I take that table, and Jill and Lou can have this one?"

Ginger nods, relieved, and follows Melissa. My stomach drops. I don't want to be left alone with

Mom. I don't know what to say to her. How do you make small talk with your mother after she becomes a stranger?

"You look good, Lou. Real good." Her voice is raspy and lower than normal, like she's caught a cold. "You've got some meat on your bones now?" It's a statement, but she says it like a question. I stay quiet.

"Is that a new jacket?" She points a red nail at the North Face that Ginger bought me in Florida. I fight the urge to tell her it was on sale. Why should I? Why should it matter? I shrug. She doesn't seem bothered that I'm not talking. Which bothers me.

When she takes off her own jacket, I spot a little round sticker on her bicep. She catches me looking and pats it.

"Nicotine patch. I'm trying to quit." She laughs then, which turns into a cough. "Amelie went and threw out all my smokes."

"Amelie got you to quit." Emphasis on "Amelie." I'd been trying to get her to stop smoking for years. Cigarettes cost more than food. But I guess Amelie has more say than her own daughter. I can feel tears start to build in the corners of my eyes. I stare into the latte until they go away.

"Yeah. I've been crashing on her couch, working shifts at Christy's." She leans forward so fast it rocks the table. "Trying to save up to get back to you, baby girl."

It sounds true. Sounds like something she would do. I can see her in black pants and a white pressed shirt at Christy's. Talking good tips off people and pocketing them in an envelope marked *Lou fund*. But something doesn't add up.

"Why didn't you just ask Ginger for money? If that was all that was keeping you away?"

She leans back now and shoots a glare over at the next table where Melissa and Ginger are politely ignoring each other by typing on their phones.

"Because I don't need a handout from my sister." She can make "sister" sound like a dirty word. Seems like taking in your only daughter is a pretty big handout to me. I push through it.

"But then we could have been together sooner. Then it wouldn't have taken *eight weeks* for you to get here."

"Lou, honey, I love you, I do. And that's why I

knew it was best for you to live with family while I got myself together." She starts peeling apart the soggy tissue on the table. "But you've got to let me do things my way in my own time."

"But it's not just about you!" I yell, because the anger that's been building for weeks now has finally sparked. I am *blazing* mad. "It's not just *your* time. It's *my* time and *Ginger's* time and *Dan's* time and you didn't even *call*!"

This was a huge mistake. Being around Mom is like being around a blaring siren. *She* is one of my triggers. I've got to get out of here. I stand with my back to her. "I'm ready to go."

"Lou, baby, don't be like that," Mom says to my back.

"Take your guitar." I nudge it away from me with my foot, still not looking at her. "I don't want it anymore." I'm waiting for Ginger, who is frozen, to get a *move* on already.

Melissa calmly checks her watch and says, "You've still got seventeen minutes. You sure you're done, Lou?"

Behind me, I hear Mom sigh.

My hands are shaking inside my pockets, and my

heart feels cracked wide open by this woman who I can't even talk to anymore.

"Yeah. I'm sure."

It's quiet in the car, just when I don't want it to be. Ginger's lost in her own thoughts about Mom. I fiddle with the radio, but there's nothing but Christmas music. I'm already sick of it, and it's just the beginning of December. Ginger keeps twisting her hands on the wheel like it's a towel she's wringing out. She's driving too slow. Old people in Cadillacs are passing us and honking. I don't say anything. I just want to get away. I don't care how long it takes to get there.

Mom's gone on the patch and got a job and saved up money. But she's still the same. She's still opinionated and pushy. I tug at my jacket zipper. How are we supposed to live together when we can't even have a conversation? Do I even *want* to live with her again? I'm confused and angry and also weirdly relieved to see that she's okay, which makes me angry all over again. I let my head rest on the cold window and close my eyes until we get home.

When we pull into the drive, I spot Well sitting

on the front steps hugging a giant trophy like a teddy bear. Ginger gets out of the car and walks inside with a tiny wave good-bye to us. Mom wasn't exactly Miss Congeniality to her, either. I can't believe she'd treat her own sister that way. Then again, it's Mom, so I guess I can.

I take a seat next to Well.

"Nice trophy."

"I'm thinking of naming her Stella." He pats it like a dog. "I'm still gonna quit next year, though." He pulls his hat down low over his ears. "How'd it go with your mom?"

Through the open door, I glimpse Dan folding Ginger up in a hug so tight I can barely see the top of her head.

"Let's take a walk," I say.

I grab a blanket from the back of the Lexus and lead Well around the house, across the lawn, through the back gate, and into the forest. He starts humming the opening lines from the play, "Into the woods," and then cannot help but sing the rest at full volume.

By the time he's done, we've made it to the little wooden bridge. The stream is lined with snowy leaves on either side. We lean on the rail, and I open the blanket to wrap it around both of us, leaving an inch or so of space between our shoulders.

"So?" he asks again.

"Mom was Mom," I say finally.

"Which means?"

"Which means I don't know how to be around her anymore. Or if I want to. She's doesn't even *know* me—not the me that's here and does theater and has friends and oh—"

"What?" he asks.

"I didn't even tell her about the *iPhone*."

"So tell her. Tell her all that stuff."

"I can't."

"Why?" He kicks a stick off the bridge and into the water. We watch it disappear behind us.

"She doesn't know about the SPD. She won't even believe it's a real thing." I sigh.

"So tell her."

I throw the blanket off.

"It's not that simple!"

"Why not?"

"You know, I don't like this version of you—this Mr. Miyagi from the *Karate Kid* version of you."

"Ohhh, look at you quoting movies at me. And an Asian reference, at that."

"Ha. Ha."

We sit down on the bridge facing each other. The snow sinks into my jeans. Well is still in his tennis shorts. He's got to be cold. How do I explain our old life, living in a truck and falling asleep to the sound of our stomachs growling, to a boy like Well, who has a theater in his basement and a credit card on file at Little Caesars?

"You don't know how we used to live. Things are too different now. I can't talk to her. It's not like talking to you or Ginger. She's a *force*, Well. A force."

Well leans toward me, too close for comfort as always. "So are you, Lou. You're like . . . a superhero who doesn't know your own strength. You just have to test it out. And who better to test it out on than your mom?"

I like the me that Well sees. But Well is good at make-believe. I picture myself turning into Wonder

Woman and lassoing Mom and holding her still until she sees me, really sees me.

"The key here," he says, leaning in close and settling the blanket back around my shoulders, "is to remember that with great power comes great responsibility."

"Wow. You actually had me up until that last bit." I throw some snow on him.

Well shrugs. His favorite move.

13
The Show Must Go On

In the dark like this, being in the middle school gym is kind of like being underwater, with nothing but the dim strips of glow-in-the-dark stage tape to light my way. Sounds are muffled. I have to fight the urge to hold my breath. I keep looking up and around for a source of light. It's the very last rehearsal, and it's not going well.

Mary Katherine *still* doesn't know all her lines, and Lacey, our Rapunzel, keeps tripping on her wig. And though I'm not going to be the one to tell him this—because Mrs. Nicky has already done it enough—Well is overacting. Big time. He keeps yelling his lines.

"Maxwell! Stop *flirting* with the crowd. *Forget* about the crowd. Sing to your wife, sing to your undiscovered child. Sing to anything that will make you wipe that smarmy car salesman look off your face!" Mrs. Nicky is having a rough night. She turns to me at our table in front of the stage. "Lou, where is Evan? We need our Prince out on stage in two minutes."

"I'll find him."

I don't have to find him. I know where he is. He's in the hallway with Mary Katherine. He is always somewhere with Mary Katherine. The only time he ever makes it onstage in time is when he's supposed to be in a scene with Mary Katherine. Unfortunately for all of us, this is not one of those scenes.

Rehearsal ends at nine. Not because it's over and perfect and we've nailed our last run-through, but because the parent's association says all extracurriculars for middle schoolers have to be over by nine, a fact that Mrs. Nicky threatens to appeal at least once every rehearsal.

"Hey, we're headed to Sonic. Want to come?"

Geneva asks on our way out to the parking lot. She's left her witch makeup on. It works on her.

"Cherry limeades and tots FOR THE WIN!" Tucker cheers. He's been working double time trying to get the set finished, which means double dinners plus snacks. They both hop in Geneva's mom's SUV, and Jacob climbs in after. Jacob has maybe the best theater job. He can hide up in his AV box away from the chaos. But it must have been a rough night for him, too, because he's got that glassy-eyed look he sometimes gets after playing too many video games.

Well lifts his eyebrows at me before stepping up onto the foot rail of their car. It's his "Whaddya say?" face. But I spot Ginger's Lexus under the glow of the farthest parking lot light.

"Nah, there's something I've got to do. Thanks, though."

"Oh, *mystery*. I'm intrigued. Tell me about it tomorrow." It's not a question, and he doesn't wait for an answer before piling in with the others. I follow their headlights all the way down the drive and really, really wish I could just go get a slushie at the drive-in instead of what I'm about to do.

Twenty minutes later, Ginger and I pull up to the Cracker Barrel off Cool Springs Boulevard. Melissa is already there, leaning against a black Camry.

I point to the car.

She shrugs. "I do sometimes have to transport kids, you know. Can't ride my bike all the time," she says, and then nods toward the porch. "Your mom's up there. Take whatever time you need. She's on a red-eye flight to California tomorrow night. This might be the last talk before your court date in a few weeks." I look at Melissa in her black leather jacket and biker boots and wonder, not for the first time, how in the world she got into social services. But I'm glad she did.

Mom's the one who called this meeting. At first I told them I couldn't go, that I had rehearsal. But Andrea talked me into it. After the botched meeting at the Good Cup, I told her I thought Mom was one of my triggers, and she said I had to approach her like that, then. Find a way to cope, work on a strategy, like a five-second rule for Mom. "Because as with any trigger," she said, "you can't just ignore it and expect it to go away." I beg to differ, but I guess we'll see.

Mom agreed to meet wherever and whenever. She said she just wanted ten minutes. I don't know what she thinks will change in that amount of time.

I walk up the steps and then down the long row of rocking chairs all decorated with Christmas bows and holly. My stomach is knotted into a complicated pattern of nerves. I briefly consider making a break for it, stealing Melissa's car, and fleeing to Sonic.

Too late. Mom spots me from where she's sitting in the very last rocker with two to-go cups in her lap. Her hair's up in a high ponytail like a teenager. She looks tiny in that big chair.

I sit down next to her. She hands me one of the cups.

"Hot chocolate."

"Thanks." I hold it but don't sip. Drinking it seems like giving in somehow.

"And look—" She pulls a green-striped candy cane from her pocket. "They had the spearmint kind. Your favorite." She starts to hand it to me and then stops, like maybe that's the wrong thing to do, and I realize she's nervous. I've never seen her nervous in my life. My stomach unknots a little.

245

"So, Ginger tells me you're in a play!"

"I'm not *in* the play. I'm helping direct. Wait. You talked to Ginger?" Since when have they made up? I grip the cup tighter. I thought Ginger was on my side.

"Yeah, we, uh, had a good chat. It was good. It's been a long time."

"Because you made it a long time."

Mom kicks off against the porch to get her chair rocking and sighs. "Yes, because I made it a long time."

"Because she wanted to help you, help *us*, get a fresh start."

You can't just smooth over the past months with hot chocolate and candy canes, I want to add. But Mom holds up a hand before I can get there.

"Listen, Lou. I know I haven't always made the right choices. *Lord,* I know that. But I thought I was doing what was best for you. You were skittish, even back then. No one but me could settle you. I thought it would be better if it was just the two of us." She twists the lid of her hot chocolate.

Skittish. Jittery. Sensitive. Shy. Mom had so many words for me, except none of them were right.

"But you left home when you were pregnant. Was I 'skittish' before I was even born?"

She sighs again. I don't care. That's what happens when you're finally allowed to ask questions after *twelve years*. It all comes out at once.

"That's a whole other ball of wax. Me and my parents had a complicated relationship. I know what it's like to grow up in that house. I didn't want that for you."

"At least we would have *had* a house."

Mom jerks her rocker to a stop. "That's enough now," she says in her old voice. The bossy one. That's better. No more fake politeness.

"You think it was an easy choice? I was basically a child myself. I want you to hear something." She leans back in her chair and starts rocking again, like she's settling in to tell me the truths of the universe. "People won't give you an inch, so you've got to take a mile. I was taught to fight my way up in this world, and that's what I wanted to teach you. You're a *fighter*, Lou."

That stupid word again.

"I have a sensory processing disorder. SPD." I spit it out. She puts her feet down to stop her chair, and

I consider running. She squints at me. Like I'm telling her a lie. Like it's a bunch of mumbo jumbo. And against *everything* I told myself before coming here, I find myself backpedaling. "That's, um, what Andrea, the counselor at school, thinks, anyway."

She starts shaking her head, and now I *really* want to run. I can't do this with her. She makes me feel so small and *wrong*. But something makes me stay. Mom's a force, but Well told me I was a force too. I'm not the same person I was two months ago, and Mom needs to hear what I have to say. There's no way forward now but through.

"SP—" she starts.

The cup shakes in my hands, but my voice is steady when I speak.

"SPD, Mom. It means crowds and loud noises and hugs and handshakes get all tangled up in my brain, and my body can't sort it out. I freak out. You already know that. You knew how it was for me. But you still made me do all those karaoke nights and shows at the fairs and farmer's markets and street corners. Mom, *why?*"

In our tiny world of two, she was always the talker

and I was the listener. I never thought to ask why until we got separated. I assumed that however hard those shows were, she was trying to do what was best for me. I don't think that anymore.

She's quiet for so long, I'm not sure what to do. I can't tell if she's mad or trying to think up an excuse or what. It's like sitting next to one of those street performers who pretend to be a statue. You wait and watch for signs of life. I can hear my own heartbeat in my ears. It's too fast.

Finally, she speaks, and it's so predictable, I'm mad I ever thought it could be different: "You have such a *gift*." I slump down in my seat, ready for the rest. "I just wanted you to see you could make it big. Really be someone great, Louise."

"I never wanted to make it big, Mom. I just wanted to be with you." It comes out ragged. I'm all fought out.

Something happens then. Something I've never seen before. Her face falls in on itself, and she starts to cry, *really* cry. She's faked it plenty of times to get out of parking tickets and stuff like that. But this is the real deal, and it makes my own throat close up, like when someone yawns and you have to do it too. I made my mom cry. She starts to reach for me, but I flinch, and she lets her arm fall in her lap.

"Oh, my baby. I am so sorry."

I swallow hard. She thinks I'm done. The big revelation is over. But she needs to hear the rest, what Andrea and I practiced in her office earlier today. But it feels even scarier to say than the SPD stuff. I'm about to take a hammer to everything that made our relationship work.

"I'm *done* with the shows, okay?"

I can't look at her after I say it. But out of the corner of my eye I see her wipe her face with a napkin. She sits, for a minute, or an eternity. I focus on the cars in the parking lot. Count the trucks. There are eight. Count the shrubs along the sidewalk. There are twelve. I feel like a spinning coin getting wobblier and wobblier and waiting to fall.

Finally she whispers, "Does that mean you want to live with me again?"

She listened. She actually listened! It shouldn't be earth-shattering, but it is. I take a sip of hot chocolate to give me a second to breathe. If she'd asked me a month ago, I wouldn't have had to think twice about it. But now all I can say is, "I—I'm not sure."

She plunges ahead. "We'd get a real apartment this time. Stay in one place. Make a real go of it."

I fiddle with my jacket zipper. This is confusing. I'm so happy she isn't going to make me sing in front of people anymore. But I'm terrified of what it'll be like, just the two of us again. I look at Ginger talking to Melissa by the front doors. What about her and Dan? What about Well and my new school?

"Can I think about it?" I whisper over my hot chocolate.

"Yes. Of course. One day at a time, baby girl."

We don't say good-bye. We don't know how. But I wave to her as Ginger and I drive away, and she waves back. I know I'll see her again in just a few weeks, but still I have to take short, quick breaths to keep from crying as she disappears in the rearview mirror.

On the way home, I take the spearmint candy out of my pocket and snap a piece off to dissolve in my mouth. I feel pretty good after our talk—hopeful even.

Like Mom and I are actually learning to talk to each other. It's not until I'm lying in bed in my blue room that night that I realize Mom never *really* answered my question. She never said we'd quit the shows.

It's Friday night—opening night.

Mary Katherine is in the bathroom with Geneva, who looks like she's about to poke Mary Katherine's eye out with a pencil. But then she tucks the pencil between her teeth and dabs at the corner of Mary Katherine's eye with her fingertip. Geneva is also our makeup person.

"Are we almost done here? My mom's just dropped off sushi," Mary Katherine whines.

Geneva might still poke her eye out yet.

"Yeah, we're done."

I let Mary Katherine, our Cinderella, brush by me in a swirl of burlap skirts. She hates this costume, the dirty rags of "Cinder" before her makeover to a princess.

"She thinks the fajitas we had catered are too heavy for her delicate stomach," Geneva says, jabbing the eye pencil into her hair like a chopstick. We roll our eyes at each other in the mirror. We don't have time to deal with Mary Katherine right now. So after Geneva draws a big unibrow and hairy mole on herself as the witch, I ask, "Are you all set?"

"Yep. I'm good. But you better check on Maxwell. He looks like he's going to puke."

I find him backstage leaning against the cardboard cutout we use for a cow.

"Hey."

"Hey," he says weakly.

"You okay?"

"I'm all right," he mutters. "I just need a minute." He's picking at his nails. They look naked without any polish. Mrs. Nicky made him take it all off for the show.

"Hey, listen—" I sit beside him against the cow. "You were great in rehearsal. Really. You know all your lines and your blocking. You'll be fine."

"Oh, I know I'm awesome. But—" He starts to run a hand through his hair, then stops because Geneva hairsprayed it up into a hard shell. "Lou, this is my first show."

"I know—it's opening night. Everybody's nervous," I say.

"No, I mean, this is my first show *ever*."

"But—"

"I know. I went *on and on* about being a thespian, but they don't let you do theater until sixth grade! So even though I've been an actor in *spirit* since forever, this is, you know, my first time being onstage."

I know this is my moment to give the big inspirational "go get 'em" talk. But I'm not Mrs. Nicky, or Well for that matter, with the speeches at the ready. I've only got one thing that might help, but I don't know if I can do it. I look at Well's pale nails, the line under his chin where the makeup stops in an awkward swipe. He's swallowing over and over again, like he might really vomit. I can't believe I'm going to do this. I'm not even sure I can. But I'm going to try.

"Okay, listen, don't get used to this, but . . . three-second firm hug, okay?"

He sits up. "Seriously?"

"Yes." My stomach churns like a million fish in a net. "Now. Do it before I change my mind."

I hold my breath. We hug, awkwardly, because he's in full makeup and I've got my headset on. And also because we are leaning against a cardboard cow.

"Better?" I say a little shakily when we let go.

He grins. "Much."

"Good." I tap my headset. "Because Mrs. Nicky's telling everyone to get in position."

I see him do another panicky swallow, but he gets up and slips behind the closed curtain to his spot, marked with an *X*. I wipe my palms on my jeans. My first big job as assistant director, *and friend*, I think, is done.

Mrs. Nicky takes the stage in front of the curtain. Tonight she has a long green silk scarf wrapped around her throat and glittery green earrings like leaves. She looks like a glamorous and slightly dangerous snake. Jacob brings the house lights down and narrows a spotlight on her.

"Ladies and gentlemen, we all walk through life wanting. Wanting to be better at something, to be loved by someone, to be seen for who we really are. Fairy tales give us hope that wrongs will be righted, the prince will come, good will win, and that there is"— she pauses for dramatic effect—"a happily ever after."

The audience starts to clap, but she holds up a hand for silence.

"*But* what does it mean to get what you want? What does the 'after' in 'happily ever after' look like?" She waits a beat. "*Into the Woods* is about magic and hope, yes. But more than that, it's about living beyond the neat ending and walking bravely into the rest of your life. And now, without further ado"—another pause—"*Into the Woods!*"

The music cues up as she makes her way gracefully offstage. I tuck myself back into the shadows and watch as the curtains open on Well as the Baker stage left and Mary Katherine in her position by a spray-painted fireplace, leaning on a broom in her Cinder rags.

"'I wish,'" Mary Katherine sings, leaning into her broom, "'I wish to go to the festival . . .'"

And we are off and running.

Act 1 goes all right with only a few minor glitches. Evan forgets his microphone is still on when he walks offstage, and the audience hears him throw his sword down and mutter, "Cheap Walmart plastic *toy* stabbed me in the leg," before I can signal Jacob to cut him off. Lacey misses a cue and enters late for her duet with

Geneva. But Well, he's perfect. The stage fright made him just subdued enough to sound genuine instead of showy. I'm so proud I could burst.

When we break for intermission, everyone gathers backstage in a sweaty heap. I find Mary Katherine with her feet in Evan's lap.

"We need you in the bathroom for your costume change," I say. Act 2 opens with Cinderella married to the Prince, but she's got to look a little worn around the edges—smudges on her cheek and her blue satin dress—the "wear and tear of married life," as Mrs. Nicky put it.

"In a minute."

This is the part I hate. The part where I have to push.

"No. Now. You have to be back onstage in five minutes."

"Lou, give her a break. She's not feeling great," Evan says, making this the first time he has ever talked to me directly. I look closer at her. She looks a little pale under her makeup, maybe even a little green.

"What's wrong?"

"Nothing. I'm fine! I'm going!" She heaves herself

up. "So you don't have to tattle to Mrs. Nicky, okay?"

Charming Cinderella.

But she's not fine. That is pretty obvious about halfway through act 2, and it becomes crystal clear when she vomits backstage with her mike still on. I rush to the bathroom. Mrs. Nicky and a few stagehands are standing over her. She's lying on her back on the tile floor, like a murder victim. And then she moans, and everyone takes a step back.

"Oh God, the sushi," she says, and curls up in a ball.

Well runs in, holding his puffy baker's hat in his hands.

"Maxwell, your services are not required. Get back outside."

"My number's over, Mrs. Nicky. I came to get the lowdown."

"Out." She points her finger and then turns to Mary Katherine, who is slowly crawling toward a bathroom stall. "*You* are not going onstage again."

"But I have to! It's my last song! I—" She throws a hand over her mouth and doesn't finish. We all exit the bathroom at a sprint.

"Lou can do it, Mrs. Nicky," Well says once the door swings shut on the sound of Mary Katherine's heaving.

"Shut up, Well!"

"What? You can!" he says, and then turns to Mrs. Nicky, who is now looking at me like she's trying to decide if I'm the right car for her. "She already knows the song."

"Shut *up*, Well." I look at the clock. Cinderella has to be back onstage in seven minutes. Our class isn't big enough for understudies. Mrs. Nicky passed out Emergen-C tablets and threatened everyone with Saturday school if they got so much as a sniffle. I can feel my heart racing. I'm getting dizzy. This is so much bigger than a three-second hug. This is a sensory nightmare.

Mrs. Nicky takes a deep breath through her nose and says in the softest voice I have ever heard her use, "Lou, this is entirely your call. I would love to see you under the lights tonight, but the show will go on. We will live to act another day with, or without, a last song from Cinderella."

Well turns to me. He's just a vague shape in front of my eyes. My vision's gone blurry with fear. "It's the duet with the Baker, Lou. With your mike on and earpiece in, you won't be able to hear anything but you and me." Well holds up his hand. "I promise."

I swallow. This means so much to him. I look at Mrs. Nicky, who's doing her best to seem like she doesn't care one way or the other. I walk several steps backward and Well starts to follow. Mrs. Nicky grabs him by the shoulder. Good. Even Well is too much company right now. Especially Well.

I turn and run for the emergency exit.

Outside it's cold. So cold my vision comes back with a snap. I'm staring at the dumpsters behind the dining hall when Tucker pushes off from the wall, sending my heart racing all over again. As a stagehand, he's in all black and truly terrifying coming out of the dark like that.

"What are you doing here?" I squeak.

"It's hot backstage, and cramped." He points to his chest. "And a guy like me doesn't do great in small spaces." His hair is damp with sweat, and his cheeks are flushed with the heat. He looks almost as miserable as I feel.

"So what do you do when we're in the middle of a scene and you can't sneak out?" I ask. Talking to him is better than thinking about what's inside right now.

He tucks his hair behind his ears and crosses his arms like he's thinking. After a minute he says, "I pretend I'm with my mom and dad, and it's hot because it's summer. Any minute we'll find a cool spot by the creek to drop a line. The heat's not so bad when you're fishing."

"And that works?"

"It works long enough to get me to the end of the scene."

We stand there in the cold for a few more seconds, our breaths making tiny locomotive clouds, and then Tucker opens the door for us to go back in.

"Thanks, Tucker."

"For what?" he asks as I slide past him.

"Just . . . thanks."

When I get back inside, Well is *right there* pacing the hallway.

"Fine," I say.

"Yeah?"

"Yeah."

It's not fine. It's *so* not fine.

"Yes!" He pumps a fist and goes running for Mrs. Nicky.

Okay. It could be worse, I tell myself backstage, and yank up my satin sleeve. I don't have to worry about the crowd. I'll be up onstage where no one can reach out and touch me. This is one of those controllable situations that Andrea is always talking about. I just have to walk on, sing one song with Well, and then walk right off again. And if worse comes to worst, I can do what Tucker does and imagine myself alone on a lake about a million miles from any living thing.

I still feel shaky, like how you get with a fever. How many Cinderellas will throw up tonight? But suddenly the lights shift from blue to amber. Mrs. Nicky herself is cueing me forward, and there's no more time to think about it. I count to three and walk onstage.

Well meets me in the center. We turn to face the audience and the spotlight sends the crowd into darkness. I say a quick prayer of thanks to Jacob for that.

I start first, and my own voice, so loud in my ears with the mike, washes over me like a peaceful wave. I take the lower part, and Well joins in a little higher. We're good together. We sing a pretty decent harmony even though we've never rehearsed. The music thrums in my chest, and it's familiar, like an old friend, from all the long rehearsals.

At one point I hear a cough from someone in the audience and have to close my eyes and picture Lake Tahoe, cold and clear and calm. It works, like Tucker said. It's enough to keep my voice steady and my feet in place. When we make our way to the very end, I feel Well next to me, readying himself for it.

On the last refrain, Well and I glance at each other, and our voices fade out together. I don't let myself look at anyone but him as the lights dim. At last, we turn and walk our separate ways offstage. When it's over, I sink to my knees in the darkness next to the cardboard cow.

"Come on! Come on! They're calling for you!" Well gestures at me like a crazed mime from across the stage after the curtain closes.

No way. Uh-uh, I mouth back, and shake my head.

Geneva runs toward me in her witch's robe with threats: "I will grab you by the arms and drag you out if you do not walk on this stage right this minute."

Tucker gives me a thumbs-up.

I feel around in my AD binder until I find the purple earplugs and stuff them in my ears. *Here goes nothing*, I think, and step out again, under the lights.

It's weird and wonderful to stand before a muffled crowd. I see them clapping, their hands moving at double speed, but they have no effect on me. It's like watching the TV with the volume on low. I see fingers in mouths, the suggestion of whistles and shouts. But it's all a distant hum. Like floating underwater. I am safe here. I turn my head to look at Well. He does not hold my hand. But we bow together.

"That was fan-freaking-tastic!" Tucker pants. He ran from backstage to congratulate me and Well and Geneva. Then everybody's there all at once—stagehands, extras, parents, Principal Myers, Andrea. Mrs. Nicky passes out daisies to the cast and crew. She pauses in front of me, kisses a daisy, and hands it to me with a whispered "thank you." Despite all my instincts, I want to give her a hug. I hug the daisy instead. She smiles and winks and walks away.

More parents walk in and teachers, and, as awesome as it is, it's a little much. I ease my way toward the bathroom, where it's quiet and thankfully doesn't smell like vomit anymore. I've just pulled back on my assistant-director gear—black jeans and sweater—when the door opens. It's Ginger and Dan . . . and Mom.

"Lou, you were great! I didn't know you were going to be *onstage*," Ginger gushes. Dan shoots me a double thumbs-up. They're grinning like I just won an Oscar.

I turn to Mom. It's instinctual to wait for her reaction after a performance. This is what we do. This is how we work. She's in a white T-shirt and plain gray blazer that I recognize as Ginger's. Her hair's up in a twist. She looks nice.

"I thought you left."

"My flight's not until eleven. I wanted to see this show my baby was directing."

"I wasn't supposed to go onstage."

"But you did."

"I did."

"And you were a star."

I don't smile.

"It was a one-time thing. I just did it to help my friends."

"Yes, but you nailed it, baby! Just think what you could—"

"Stop!" I yell, because it's the only way to make her listen. "Just stop!"

I push through the door and out into the lobby and out again onto the snow-dusted lawn behind the dining hall. I sit down on a picnic table and wrap my arms around myself. My new jacket's back in the bathroom. I breathe fast in little, uneven huffs. Leave it to Mom to ruin this for me.

I hear steps crunching over the frozen grass behind me. Someone puts a hand as gentle as a feather on my back. I know it's Mom without looking, because even as upset as I am, my body still accepts her touch.

"Lou—"

"I don't want to talk to you."

"Lou, I'm sorry."

She sits down next to me and hands me my jacket.

"You're always sorry. It never changes anything."

I pull the jacket over my shoulders and let it be the thing that knocks her hand away. She starts wiping snow off the picnic table like it's her job to clean it.

"You're right. My apologies aren't worth much. But, baby, I just got so excited! And I *am* trying. I'm not good at having to share you. It's been you and me against the world for so long."

"But I don't want that anymore." I sniff and look for something to wipe my nose with. Mom hands me a tissue.

"I know," she says finally, and she rubs her knuckles. They're cracked and dry.

"We can't do it anymore by ourselves, Mom. And I don't want to 'make it big.' I just want to be normal, or my version of normal, anyway. I have friends now and I do go to school and yeah, I still sing sometimes, because I'll always love music. But it's when *I* want to, and it's not for anyone but me."

"I get it."

"Do you?"

She looks at me. We have the same hazel eyes.

"Yes, I do. And I promise on our old beat-up truck, which is still alive and kicking, by the way, that I will not make you do another gig."

"Swear on your favorite rhinestone jacket."

"I'll do you one better." She puts her hand over her heart, and her red nails flash under the streetlight. "I swear on my heart."

Something like hope rises with my next breath when she says, "Now tell me about your friends."

I tell her about Well and Geneva and Tucker and Jacob. And I tell her about my A in English and Mrs. Nicky's rumba and Dan's crossword puzzles and Ginger's terrible tomato juice.

When we walk back inside, I spot Well and wave, but before I can get to him, his dad steps in. He's in a shiny shirt and jeans and smells like he's been hit by a tidal wave of aftershave. "Maxwell didn't tell me you were a singer," he says, holding a card up between two fingers, so close to my face I have to take it or get stabbed in the eye. I study the card: WRIGHT MANAGE-

MENT is embossed on the front next to a giant gold music note. "Call me," he barks. It sounds like an order. Behind him, Well rolls his eyes.

"Thank you, sir," I say, sweet as apple pie. Mom, for once, is silent. When he walks away, she watches me throw the card in a trash can without a word.

"Brava," Well says, and claps.

14
Auld Lang Syne

Ginger hung tinsel and twinkle lights from every sconce and light fixture in the house. And she cooked. Well . . . she heated up pigs in a blanket and mini quiches, her version of cooking.

It's eleven forty-five p.m. Fifteen minutes to midnight on New Year's Eve and everybody who's anybody is here, meaning Ginger and Dan and Well and Geneva and Tucker and Jacob and Mom. Mom brought a cheesecake that she made from scratch in the kitchen of her new apartment. Who knew my mom could cook? She's in the kitchen now, sitting on the counter and eating that cheesecake right off the serving platter with Ginger. We all played Scrabble until Dan had to take a time-out after Jacob played "xu" for twenty-seven points. I tried Jenga with Geneva, but it was a little too stressful. Currently, I'm trying not to fall asleep in the corner of the sofa.

We got back from Tahoe yesterday. Mom and Ginger and Dan and I flew out for the court hearing. I didn't melt down on the plane. But I did turn the music up so loud my ears rang for an hour after we landed. Maria met us at the airport. Because I have the iPhone now, I gave her back the iPod and told her to pass it on to another kid who needed it.

Tahoe in December was exactly like a postcard. Snow everywhere. Big old-fashioned Christmas lights strung on all the ski lodges and pubs and pizza places. Icicles clinging to the pines. The water was still that same clear blue with the mountains standing watch in the distance. We stopped in at Joe's for lox-and-cream-cheese bagels and the biggest latte he could make. He still didn't let us pay.

When the judge, an older lady with bright red

cat's-eye glasses and a neat bob, asked me what I wanted to do, whether I thought it would be better to live with Mom or stay with Dan and Ginger, I knew whatever I said wasn't going to be the final call. Melissa and Maria had already explained that my testimony was just one of the pieces of the puzzle. But still, I wanted to be honest and to say what I'd been thinking as best I could.

I stood in the front row of the tiny courtroom with wood-paneled walls and creaky benches and said, "I know my mom and I weren't living so great there for a while, and I know she made some mistakes and I shouldn't have been driving that truck. Sorry about that, ma'am."

The judge smiled and nodded for me to go on.

"I'm so grateful I got to meet my aunt Ginger and uncle Dan. They gave me my first real home and put me in a school that I actually really like. So I don't want to go back to not seeing them again.

"But"—I took a breath—"my mom's my mom. I can't picture not seeing *her*, either. She's got a new apartment, and she's working at a coffee shop in

Nashville. She's doing okay. The thing is . . . I don't want to pick between Mom and Dan and Ginger. I want everybody."

Maybe the judge already had her decision made. But when she read her ruling, I can't help but think it was something I said that tipped the scales. So, yeah, I'm staying with Dan and Ginger for now. Maybe, if Mom can keep her job and her promise to go with me to all my OT appointments and not so much as *suggest* an open-mike night, then we can talk about our living arrangements again this summer. But for now, I get to finish the school year at Chickering. Mom even agreed to let Dan and Ginger pay my tuition, which is proof that miracles do happen. I get to keep my mom, my aunt, my uncle, my friends, *and* my school. It seems like too much good all at once for one person, but I'll take it.

"Come on. Do it."

"No."

Well leans over from his end of the couch. He's in a powder-blue tuxedo and top hat. He said he saw it in a movie once. His nails are silver.

"For old times' sake?"

"No."

"For New Year's sake?"

"No."

"For my sake?" He takes off his top hat and holds it to his chest. I fiddle with the silver tassels along the hem of my dress. It's a 1920s flapper dress that Mom found at a thrift store. I kind of love it.

"Fine."

"Don't sound too excited."

"Three more seconds and I'm taking it back."

"Okay, okay!"

When the countdown begins and the ball drops, I plug my ears with my fingers. But when it hits the big flashing 2021, Ginger hushes everybody, and Mom whips out her old guitar in the center of the room. I let my hands fall to my sides and take my place next to Well in front of the fireplace.

He hums a key, she counts us off, and I begin:

"'Should old acquaintance be forgot . . .'"

"Auld Lang Syne" is a beautiful song to sing with old and new friends. I take it nice and slow and let the rumbling in my chest carry it forward. Of course, Well joins in like he's Justin Timberlake and sends it into hyperspeed, but whatever, that's Well.

I match his pace, and we rock it out, Mom playing for all she's worth. Then it's a giant game of musical chairs as everybody runs to toast everybody else. The rest of the song kind of falls apart because we can't stop laughing. When it's over, we bow, and Tucker and Geneva and Jacob hold up signs with *APPLAUSE!* written in glittery marker. Everybody mimes clapping. Well tips his hat to me and winks.

If there *is* a more normal version of the world out there, it can't be better than this.

Acknowledgments

If you could rate your editors on Goodreads, Reka Simonsen and Julia McCarthy at Atheneum Books for Young Readers would get five stars. Thank you both for helping Lou find her way and for keeping my fictional days and coffee shops straight.

Agents should get stars too. Keely Boeving, you keep me grounded, and your first reactions to Well were priceless. Thanks for loving these characters as much as I do.

To my fellow Nashville MG writer, Kristin Tubb, you read the first five pages of this before we ever knew each other, and your encouragement was much needed and much appreciated. I'm so glad I'm an *S* and you're a *T* so we can sit together at all the festivals.

I love research! But it can only get you so far before you need to call in the experts. Special thanks go to my early readers, Stacey Steinberg and Kate Forest, for lending their knowledge of the foster care system and the Department of Children's Services. And to Katy Dieckhaus, for her wisdom and insight into working with children with sensory processing disorders.

Celia Krampien, your talents as a cover artist are beyond compare. Thank you for getting Lou just right and for creating a cover for this book that is so beautiful it sings.

Dear children of mine, Charlie, Jonas, and Cora: None of you were in school yet when this book was written. Thanks for playing nicely so I could do it. I promise to make you cinnamon rolls every Saturday for the rest of your lives.

Dear husband of mine: Thanks for marrying this theater girl and appreciating my drama. If you wondered how I became the plot-whisperer, now you know.

A special note to the teachers and librarians: thank you for championing my storytelling from the very beginning! Your support for *Roll with It* has made me braver as a writer. I am so grateful to you for getting my stories into the hands of the kids who need them and for working tirelessly in the classroom every single day.

Lastly, this book is for the kids living with invisible disabilities. I see you. You are not alone. Here's a not-so-secret secret: we're all still figuring ourselves out. Remember, there is no normal.